Dear Reader,

I've long held a dream of owning and running a bookstore in a small town. A few years ago, when my husband and I heard our favorite bookshop in our little mountain village was for sale, we seriously considered buying it. What could be more perfect, we reasoned, for an author and a soon-to-be-retired history teacher? As it turned out, the shop sold before we made a decision and the idea of owning a bookshop remained a dream.

When the opportunity came along to write *By Word of Mouth*, I was thrilled. Now I could "live" my dream and enjoy every minute of the writing process while doing so. Mary's Mystery Bookshop quickly became my own. I understood Mary's love for the shop, her passion for books, and her delight in her customers and friends who dropped by. When Betty used her teapot collection to create her after-Christmas window display, I described my own collection, down to my favorite Mary Engelbreit, an anniversary gift from my husband.

As I wrote this book, the characters came to life, becoming almost as close as my own family and friends. I love the way Mary and her sister Betty care for each other. Their relationship reminds me of how God brings others—close friends or family members—into our lives just when we need them most, to reflect His love to us, to help us on our life journeys.

I hope you enjoy reading *By Word of Mouth* as much as I enjoyed writing it. May the characters in Ivy Bay remain in your heart long after the last page is turned.

Blessings,
Diane Noble

SECRETS *of* MARY'S
BOOKSHOP

By Word of Mouth

Diane Noble

Guideposts
New York, New York

Secrets of Mary's Bookshop is a trademark of Guideposts.

Published by Guideposts
16 E. 34th St.
New York, NY 10016
Guideposts.org

Acknowledgments

Every attempt has been made to credit the sources of copyrighted material used in this book. If any such acknowledgment has been inadvertently omitted or miscredited, receipt of such information would be appreciated.

"From the Guideposts Archives" originally appeared in *Guideposts*. Copyright © 1982 by Guideposts. All rights reserved.

Cover and interior design by Müllerhaus
Cover art by Ross Jones at Deborah Wolfe LTD
Typeset by Aptara, Inc.

Printed and bound in the United States of America
10 9 8 7 6 5 4 3 2 1

ONE

The heavenly scent of fresh-baked oatmeal cookies filled Mary Fisher's home with the aroma of cinnamon and nutmeg. Outside, in the deepening dusk, a cold wind rattled the leafless elm branches against the shutters, telling of the coming storm. But inside the brightly lit home that Mary shared with her sister Betty a sense of tangible love wafted throughout the house, made stronger with each tray of cookies Betty pulled from the oven.

Mary, sitting at their small kitchen table, tried not to think about the phone call she was expecting, and instead breathed in the fresh-baked sweetness and then sighed as her spirits calmed.

The timer chimed, and her sister came through the kitchen doorway and headed to the stove. She grabbed a pot holder and pulled the tray from the oven.

"How about a sample?"

"I'd love nothing better." Mary grinned as her sister brought over a plateful, placed it between them on the table, and then went back to the counter for a couple of napkins.

As she moved, Mary could see that the chilly weather was taking its toll on Betty's swollen joints; she moved slower than usual this evening. But her uncomplaining spirit touched Mary's heart, and it made her cookie contribution to tonight's Winter Warmth Book Chat even more meaningful.

"Have you heard anything from the antiques dealer yet?" Betty eased herself into the chair on the opposite side of the table.

Mary shook her head. "He called earlier and said he might have news by closing tonight, but so far, nothing." She glanced at the clock, trying to keep her hopes up. "I'm so eager to hear, especially after my visit with Isabella today. That little girl is so brave, so full of life and laughter.... It hurts to think she has chronic kidney disease and that the only thing that will save her is a transplant."

Betty reached for Mary's hand and patted it—a gesture that reminded her Betty cared as much as she did about the little granddaughter of Bob Hiller, the neighborhood mailman. "I know that makes waiting for the phone call even harder."

Mary nodded, thinking about the brave little girl and her parents. "Yes, it does."

"Is there any news about a kidney donor?"

"They've got a good match, but there's still the issue of cost." Mary tried not to think how much was riding on the phone call she expected. After all, God was in control. If He knew when even a sparrow fell, He certainly knew the needs of this precious child and her parents.

Betty picked up the plate of cookies and held it toward Mary. "You haven't taken a bite. I'm counting on you to tell me what you think," she encouraged gently. Her eyes said she knew what Mary was feeling. "This is a new recipe."

Mary reached for a cookie, took a bite, and then she chewed thoughtfully. "You've done it this time, Bets. It's the best ever."

Betty nodded her thanks and then said, as if reading Mary's mind, "God's never failed us yet."

"It's my impatience that gets in the way of trust. I know He's in control; I feel it in my heart"—she paused, thinking about how many times she'd found this to be true—"but it's my head that forgets." She grinned. "It's a good thing He loves us just as we are and doesn't have to wait for us to always get it right to bless us."

Betty chuckled. "Well, my goodness, how did we get from a discussion of cookies to theology?"

Mary laughed. "Because of a certain little girl with huge needs, a heavenly Father who loves her more than we ever could, or even her parents could…and a phone call that could change everything." She paused. "Well, maybe not everything. But a lot."

After a few minutes, Mary gathered up her notes, placed her cell phone on top of the stack, which she left on the table, and then she stood to take the empty plate to the sink. Betty remained seated.

"By the way," Mary said as she rinsed the plate, "what are your secret ingredients? I may want to borrow the combo for a new ice cream recipe come summer."

"Butterscotch chips, a dash of almond extract, and just a pinch of grated, candied ginger—"

From where she'd left it on the table, Mary's cell phone rang. It startled them both.

"I'll get it...," Betty said, then answered and listened for a moment. "No, I'm sorry. This is her sister Betty, but she's right here....Yes, of course, yes, I'll tell her." Betty's smile spread as she handed the phone to Mary. "It's Orris Rathburn," Betty whispered.

Mary's heart pounded as she took the phone. "Hello, Mr. Rathburn," she said shakily. "It's good to hear from you."

She listened with growing astonishment as he went through the details of the offer that had come in for her book.

Betty stood across from her, smiling and nodding as if she understood every word.

"The book is worth how much?" Phone still to her ear, Mary thought her legs might give out on the spot. She practically fell into her chair. She grabbed a pen and her notebook. "Say that again. Please."

The Weston antiques dealer gave her the number. For a moment, she forgot to breathe.

"I'm sorry," she said. "I must have misunderstood. I thought I heard you say..." Her voice broke off; she couldn't even utter the words.

Orris Rathburn chuckled and repeated the astonishing number. "Yes, $31,000 for *The Murder of Roger Ackroyd* by Agatha Christie, and that's after I deduct my commission. I had an idea it might be worth this much when we first spoke. But I just today received my report from the appraiser. And even better news. I found a buyer willing to pay top dollar, but he would like to send a special courier for it by noon tomorrow. He will wire the money to your account as soon as the book is once again authenticated—this time by his personal appraiser. Of course, this decision is up to you.

You can keep it on the market and see if a better offer comes along." He laughed lightly, obviously delighted with his news. "But as they say, a bird in hand is..." He chuckled again. "Well, you know the rest. Sleep on it, if you like, and let me know in the morning."

"I don't think that will be necessary," Mary said shakily. This was more, far more, than she had hoped or prayed for. Her eyes filled and her heart felt light enough to dance. *Thank You, Lord. Thank You!*

The image of Isabella Hiller danced into her mind, quickly followed by images of Isabella's mom and dad, who needed the money desperately for their sick child.

"Mrs. Fisher, are you still there?" Orris Rathburn's voice brought her back to the conversation at hand.

"Yes, I'm here," she said. "It's just that this is so unexpected.... And I'm so...glad. You see, there's this little girl who's in the hospital, and her parents—" She stopped and laughed lightly. "I'll save the details for another time. Let me just say, this money will make all the difference in the world for one dear family." She felt her eyes fill again and blinked back tears.

Rathburn was silent for a moment. When he spoke, his tone was solemn. "Then it's a double blessing to have this happen so quickly. I'm glad I could be the bearer of such good news."

"Yes," Mary said, "I am too, and thank you."

They spoke for a few minutes about the sale details, and then just before ending the call, he said, "Now that we know the value, I want to caution you about taking great care of the book." He cleared his throat. "Not that you wouldn't anyway. I don't mean to offend...."

"No offense taken. I understand. The book will remain under lock and key in my shop. I'm not worried, though; no one here knows its value. And Ivy Bay is a town full of trustworthy friends and neighbors. We're a sleepy little fishing town, especially this time of year."

"I know Ivy Bay well," he said, "and you're right about the friendly townspeople. But you never know...." He let the sentence hang, then added, "Only a few individuals in my company know anything about the book's value. That is, besides the buyer, of course."

"Thank you for the word of caution," Mary said pleasantly. "It's certainly worth paying close attention. Your courier will be here tomorrow, correct?"

"By noon."

Mary ended the call, unable to stop smiling. This time the following day, the book would be sold, the Hillers would have the needed funds to ease their financial burden, and little Isabella could possibly be on her way to Boston Children's Hospital for her much-needed surgery.

Betty's own joy was evident in her expression. "I take it Mr. Rathburn had good news."

Mary's smile widened. "The best. He's already found a buyer. You'll never guess what the buyer has agreed to pay."

Betty laughed. "I can see by your expression that it's much more than the thirty-five cents you paid at the flea market."

Mary's laughter bubbled up again. "Would you believe $31,000?"

Betty sat back, obviously stunned. She let out a delicate and ladylike whoosh of air. "Oh my," she finally said.

"Oh my, indeed." Mary couldn't stop smiling. "To think how that money will help the Hillers. And how we prayed we'd find a way." She shook her head slowly. "I'm still trying to take it all in."

"It sounded like he cautioned you about something at the end...."

"He did," Mary said, "about making sure it's safe until the courier gets here. But no one knows the book's value. It's in the locked case with my other rare books, and no one has ever seemed overly interested in those."

Betty went back to the counter, gave the dough a stir, and as she dropped dollops on a cookie sheet, she said, "No doubt about it, Ivy Bay is a wonderful and safe place to live."

Mary frowned. "Why do I have the feeling you're about to add a 'but'?"

"We have had our share of pranks and the odd thing happening now and again."

Mary remembered the break-in that happened when she first opened her shop and took a deep breath. "That's true," she said. "But in this case, with no one aware of the book's value, there really shouldn't be anything to worry about."

Betty smiled again. "Of course. But I also know how news travels in this community. It's strange. Somehow the word gets out, and before you know it, the whole town finds out about something you had no idea had gotten out in the first place." She paused, her thoughtful gaze resting on Mary. "Just take extra care."

"I will. A lot is riding on this sale," Mary said, a bit of nervousness now crowding in with her elation. "I think I'll leave early for the book chat just to make sure everything is secure."

She went down the mental list of security measures. The case that contained her rare books was locked; the shop was locked. She trusted her employee Rebecca to care for the bookshop and its books as if they were her own. She reminded herself that there was no need to jump to conclusions, to "borrow trouble" as her mother used to say.

TWO

It didn't take long for Mary to gather up her notepad and notes for the Winter Warmth Book Chat, which was due to meet in her bookshop in an hour. The book chat was the brainchild of a talk that Betty and Mary had in the bookshop one day just after Christmas. The scent of baking cinnamon rolls and apple pies had drifted in from Sweet Susan's next door, and several customers had been lamenting that the holidays—including the copious baking that happened at Thanksgiving and Christmastime—were over and they had nothing but cold weather to look forward to.

"It doesn't need to be that way," Mary had said to Betty after the shop had closed. Betty had come by after hours to plan out her next window display.

Betty had grinned, a twinkle in her eye. "Not at all. Especially the baking."

"And the books," Mary said. "There's nothing like curling up with a good mystery in front of the fireplace on a cold winter's night."

It was as if they'd read each other's minds. "Let's call it the Winter Warmth Book Chat," Betty said, clapping her hands decisively. "We'll have tea and homemade cookies. It won't be a formal, weekly sort of thing. Not after the busyness of the holidays."

"Right. Not a formal book club at all. We'll just meet when the spirit moves us," Mary said, smiling with her. "Decide ahead of time, of course, what we'll read. How about *Murder on the Orient Express* for the first book, to kick things off? Nothing better than a classic Agatha Christie."

"Sounds perfect. And I've already got the window design in mind." Betty walked over to the Christmas display. "It's time to renew and revamp." She turned, her eyes still bright. "I've been dying to get out my teapot collection, and this is the perfect excuse. Nothing says winter warmth and comfort like a hot pot of tea."

"That sounds like just the thing," Mary said. "And I'll put up a sign-up sheet. Find out who's interested. Let's just see what happens."

And here it was, little more than a week later and time for the first meeting. At least a dozen had signed up, but with the blustery weather outside, she knew some might not venture out.

Mary glanced at the clock as she slipped her arms into her full-length down coat and then wrapped a long woolen scarf around her neck and pulled on her leather gloves.

"You're sure you wouldn't like for me to wait for you?" She watched Betty slide another baking sheet filled with dollops of cookie dough into the oven.

Betty turned and gave her a half smile. "I didn't mean to alarm you, but I really think it's wise to take extra care."

"I agree completely." Another whistling burst of wind rattled the windows. "But I also don't like the idea of you driving alone in this—even if it is such a short distance."

Betty looked up at her, quirked a brow, and then laughed. "Mar, don't forget how long we've both lived on this coast." She straightened, closed the oven door, and turned, her expression serious. "I heard the forecast earlier. We've got some brisk winds blowing in ahead of the storm. Watch for downed branches, blowing sand, that sort of thing. I'll be along as soon as I finish baking this last batch."

Mary smiled at her sister's concern about the forecast. It reminded her of something John would have said. As she grabbed her purse, she thought about how much Betty had given of herself since Mary's arrival as a new widow, still grieving over her husband's death. Betty had been there for her and understood, having lost her own husband Edward too. And she had opened her home to Mary, making it clear she wanted Mary to consider it her own.

"Thanks again for baking the cookies."

Betty set the timer. "That was the idea, right? Warm, gooey cookies, accompanied by Agatha Christie. I can't wait to chat about the book!"

"Me neither," Mary said with a laugh. "I love the book, and, of course, I also love that there's so much mystery surrounding Miss Christie herself."

"You mean her disappearance."

Mary nodded. "Yes, and never solved. But I'm sure we'll get to that during the chat!"

A moment later, Mary slid behind the steering wheel of her Impala. As she waited for the engine to warm, she glanced at her sister's house. The lamps in the windows cast a warm, friendly glow into the blustery night. And the twinkling lights outlining the roof, still up from Christmas, added a festive look to the beautiful old house. She still felt incredibly blessed that this house was now her home.

Mary drove away, whispering a prayer of thanksgiving for her sister.

A blast of wind buffeted the car, and Mary tightened her grip on the steering wheel and slowed to a crawl to stay on the road. As she rounded the corner and started down Main Street, another gust hit head-on, and she squeezed the steering wheel even tighter. By the time she parked in front of the bookshop, the gusts had increased. She looked toward the bay and lifted her eyes to the night sky. In the thin light from a sliver of moon, she could see an ominous buildup of clouds. As she watched, the moon dipped beneath the gathering of clouds.

It was now pitch-dark, and hers was one of the only vehicles on the street. As she stepped out of the car, the icy wind stung her cheeks. Grasping her handbag and holding on to her scarf, she hurried to the front entrance. It took only seconds to reach the door, unlock it, and step inside. The little bell chimed. A small thing, but a welcome, familiar sound in the midst of the noisy wind.

Gus's rumbling purr greeted her even before she flipped on the light. Knowing she'd be back this evening, she'd left him at the shop when she locked up that afternoon. His comforting presence always cheered and calmed her.

"Hi, buddy." Mary stooped to pet him, which made him rev up the decibels on the purring scale. She chuckled and, after a couple more pats on his head, she stood, flipped on the rest of the lights, and hurried to the rear of the shop to turn on the gas fireplace. The flames shot up, adding warmth to the room.

She thought Gus would curl up and enjoy the warmth, but instead he walked back toward the front of the shop and hopped onto the glass counter. Still purring loudly, he sat above the place where she'd left the rare book. Curious, Mary headed to the counter—and the case where she kept her collection. Even before she removed the key from her handbag, she knew something was amiss.

She stared through the glass case at the nondescript cardboard box containing the rare, irreplaceable 1926 book— *The Murder of Roger Ackroyd* by Agatha Christie. The box was there, but someone had opened it. She blinked in disbelief. Just this afternoon, she had carefully wrapped the book in a special acid-free tissue paper, folded the edges, and then placed it in acid-free padding.

She glanced up at Gus who, still sitting on the counter, was now preening his whiskers. "If you could only talk…," she whispered, turning her attention again to the mess inside the case.

The lid had been tossed to one side, the padding strewn outside the box. The tissue paper was wrinkled as if someone had lifted the book to examine it and then hurriedly returned it to its box. Another thought hit her. Perhaps someone replaced the original with another book.

Surely not! That possibility spurred her into action. In simple dollars, this particular edition was worth far more than every other book in her shop.

She tried to ignore her rapidly beating heart as, hand shaking, she placed the key in the lock, only to discover it was already unlocked.

She distinctly remembered locking it before she left. How could this be? She reached inside, picked up the box, and brought it to her lap. Opening the tissue, she stared at the book. It was leather bound, in pristine condition, the title embossed in gold—a few places that looked worn with light scratches, just as she'd noted before.

It had to be the right book. But was it? There was only one way to find out.

Holding her breath, she gently opened the cover.

And then thumbed to the title page. Agatha Christie's signature was in place, just as it should have been. She then thumbed to the back cover. The author's handwritten notes outlining her next book were there, notes that Orris had said increased the value of this rare book a hundredfold.

She sat back, her hands trembling as she clutched the book to her chest.

Who had tampered with it, and why?

Mary frowned as she tried to think of a logical answer to her question.

Outdoors, the wind kicked up. In the back of the shop, the fireplace suddenly didn't seem quite as cheery, with the flames' flickering shadows on the walls, the shelves, the book spines. Glancing around, she shivered.

Tampering?

This was more than that. Her breath caught in her throat. Had she interrupted a robbery in progress? That would explain why the glass case was open, the book's packaging askew, the book itself still in place.

At once, awareness of her vulnerability swept over her, and she glanced around the shop again. What if someone had been in the shop as she had parked? She had been so busy looking up at the night sky, the sliver of a moon, and the building storm clouds, she hadn't even glanced into the shop windows. But if someone had broken in with the intent to take the book, even if they'd seen her drive up, wouldn't they have grabbed the book and made a run for the back door?

She recounted her first moments in the shop tonight; she hadn't heard anything but Gus's purring. She'd seen no flashlight beam. She'd heard no footsteps or doors closing.

Could someone still be in the shop?

Perhaps in the back room near the back door? Or in the cellar?

Her heart thudded as she lifted Gus into her arms and cautiously moved toward the rear of the shop. The fire crackled and sparked in the fireplace, and she whispered Psalm 56:3–4 to give her courage: "When I am afraid, I will trust in you. In God whose word I praise, in God I trust; I will not be afraid."

She reached the doorway of the back room and called out in a loud voice, sounding much braver than she felt, "Hello? Is anyone there?"

The only answer was another gust of wind that rattled leafless branches. Other than that, silence. She peered around the door as she flipped on the light. It was just as she'd left it when she closed the shop at the end of the workday.

She glanced at the closed cellar door, the hairs on the back of her neck standing on end. What if the would-be thief had seen her headlights, scurried to the back of the shop, run down the cellar steps, and hidden somewhere in the darkness?

No way would she descend those stairs to check. So tiptoeing toward the cellar door, she made sure it was locked and stepped away.

She set Gus on the floor and drew in a deep breath. For now, she was safe. There was still the mystery of the tampering with the book, but it was also safe.

Besides, there had to be a logical explanation. Rebecca had helped her in the shop that afternoon. Perhaps she had pulled it out to show a curious customer. She knew that Mary was having the book appraised but had no idea of its value, so she probably didn't think it would hurt. If she did show it to someone at all.

But the messy state of the box and the tissue? That wasn't at all like Rebecca.

In any case, she would check with her employee as soon as she arrived for the book chat.

Furthermore, as she had told Orris Rathburn earlier, this was Ivy Bay. She had no reason to fear. But even as the thought took hold, she shivered again.

The best thing would be to get her mind off the what-ifs and onto what she needed to do to get ready for the book chat.

She glanced around, her gaze landing on the refreshment table. She would start there. She made a mental note to ask Henry Woodrow to help with the folding chairs as soon as he arrived. And of course, they needed hot water for tea and cocoa. And the coffeemaker needed to be filled. She reached up into an overhead cupboard for the oversize coffeemaker, set it on the counter and filled it with water. Then she carried it to the refreshment table. She had just finished scooping coffee into the holder and was reaching behind the table to plug it in, Gus winding himself around her ankles, when a loud bang reverberated through the shop.

She jumped. But not half as high as Gus did. They both turned toward the noise.

The back door! Why hadn't she checked to see if it was locked? Had someone been inside, after all? The mere thought turned her knees to jelly.

She raced to the front counter where she'd left her cell phone. With trembling fingers, she punched in Henry's number.

Before she could hit Send, the back door creaked open. After a moment that seemed like an eternity, it slammed shut again.

A couple of books thumped to the floor as Gus scrambled across bookshelves, heading for higher ground.

Fingers shaking, she managed to call Henry. He answered on the first ring.

"Henry," she whispered, staring at the doorway that led to the storeroom. "I'm at the shop. Can you please come?"

"Of course," he said. "I'd planned to leave in just a few minutes, anyway."

"Oh, good. And Henry? Please hurry."

THREE

Mary was relieved when Henry arrived. He'd been her dear friend throughout her childhood summers in Ivy Bay, and when she returned after John's passing, their friendship had been renewed. Just having his solid presence with her here tonight lifted her spirits.

"Are you all right?" His concern showed in his expression as he looked down at her.

"Yes..." Mary took a deep breath. She laughed a bit nervously and then told him about Orris Rathburn's phone call, the value of the book, then finding the open glass case when she arrived at the bookshop. "And when the door slammed, I nearly jumped through the roof."

"Maybe it's just a coincidence," Henry said as he examined the back door. "Could you have forgotten to pull it all the way closed?"

"I suppose, but Rebecca closed up for me tonight. She's as careful as I am about making sure everything is locked when she leaves." Mary shook her head. "I'll ask her, of course, when I see her tonight, but I am almost certain she wouldn't have left anything unlocked."

"The book's value does put a different spin on things." Henry rubbed the doorjamb with his fingertips. "There doesn't seem to be any sign of forced entry." When he met her gaze again, her cheeks warmed at the concern she saw written in his expression.

"Which leaves this a complete mystery," Mary said. "Not that it wasn't before. How would anyone know about the book's value when I just found out myself no more than a couple of hours ago?"

Henry nodded thoughtfully. "I do think you need to call Chief McArthur with this. Maybe he can shed some light on it."

Mary hesitated, wondering if there was enough evidence to go on. She would feel terrible if she called on the police chief to investigate when other law-enforcement duties vied for his attention. "There really hasn't been a crime committed. Nothing was taken. No signs of a break-in. Just an open door and unlocked case..."

Henry quirked a brow. "And a rare, very expensive book disturbed."

"True."

Henry chuckled. "I think you should make the call." His expression sobered. "What worries me more than anything is that it's possible the would-be thief saw you drive up and then took off out the back before you had a chance to turn on the shop lights. If he hadn't run, you could have entered and..." He searched her eyes, his own showing even more worry over her.

She smiled. "If indeed he is a he and he is a thief, he did leave, and I'm fine. At least I will be once we're set up for our first ever Winter Warmth Book Chat."

She stooped to once more check the doorknob and dead bolt, still worried about bothering Chief McArthur when nothing was actually taken and the door might have slammed because of the wind.

But Henry was right. It was prudent to call the police, and also Rebecca to see if she'd taken the book out for any reason. The book was too important to leave anything to chance.

She grinned at Henry, who was holding out his cell phone. She took it from him. "Rebecca first," she said. "There may be a simple answer, and we won't need to bother the chief."

He nodded in agreement.

But when she punched in the number, it rang several times before going to voice mail.

With a sigh, she made the call to the police station while Henry headed to the cellar to bring up extra folding chairs. She called the nonemergency number and was asked if she could hold. She agreed, and phone to ear, Mary walked back to the front of the shop just as Betty drove up and parked behind the Impala.

Betty came into the shop, bearing a Tupperware case of cookies, just as the police dispatcher answered.

"We've had a possible break-in at Mary's Mystery Bookshop," she told the dispatcher, who then asked a few questions.

A few minutes later, Mary ended the call, feeling a bit dismayed. This brought back the memory of the first time her shop was broken into. Her frustration must have showed.

Betty looked shaken. "Are you all right?"

Mary gave her a reassuring smile. "I'm still not certain anyone was here. I need to check with Rebecca about the open counter and the book packaging mess. I tried to call, but she didn't pick up." She managed a reassuring smile. "She'll be here before long, anyway."

"Do you want me to straighten it up?" Betty asked.

Mary shook her head. As much as she disliked doing so, she needed to leave the book and the packaging contents as they were. "I'm sure Chief McArthur will want things left as I found them—though I did pick up the book and thumb through it."

"Is he coming over?"

Mary shook her head. "The dispatcher said the winds are causing some road problems. There are also some traffic accidents north of here, and even our off-duty officers have been called into work. Since nothing was taken from the shop and no one was hurt, it's dropped fairly low on the priority list."

She glanced down at the case and the box containing the book. If she had interrupted a robbery, she was glad. It would have been better not to have happened at all, but given what money the book would go for, and given that the robber could have taken the book and been halfway to Boston by now…she was relieved. Yes, she'd take interrupting the robbery over the book's disappearance any day.

While Henry brought up some folding chairs from downstairs, Mary helped Betty with the cookies and the rest of the accoutrements for the refreshment table. By the time they'd finished, Rebecca had arrived. She shrugged off her multicolored parka at the door and quickly stepped aside so that Bob Hiller could get in out of the cold wind.

Rebecca, dressed in a long, slightly oversized brown woolen skirt and roomy sweater, drew Mary to one side. "I hope it's all right that I invited my Great-aunt Millicent." She smiled, her pleasure at her aunt's pending visit showing in her dark brown eyes. "She's driving in from Gloucester. She's been listening to the weather news on the radio and said there are already power outages and traffic problems from the winds. But she's hoping to make it, anyway."

"We'll love having her," Mary said.

"Thank you. She loves Agatha Christie, so I invited her to the chat. She said she wasn't too far from town, but it's been a bear of a drive for her, even in her SUV." Rebecca began to pull her brown hair into a loose ponytail. "She's in her early eighties, if you can imagine. In my opinion, she should have waited, but she's been so lonely since my great-uncle Oliver died that she couldn't wait to come down to be with us."

"I understand only too well how she feels. We'll make her feel very welcome," Mary said, pointing out a stray strand of hair that hadn't made its way into the tie. Rebecca smiled and pulled the piece in. In many ways, Mary saw Rebecca and her daughter Ashley as surrogate family, while her two children— Jack and Lizzie—raised their own kids a good distance away, Lizzie in the Boston suburbs and Jack in Chicago.

Mary and Rebecca were standing near the counter, and Rebecca glanced down at the rare books and saw the packing materials, the open box, and *The Murder of Roger Ackroyd* beside it. Her shock was evident.

"What happened?"

Mary let out a breath she hadn't realized was waiting for release. It was obvious Rebecca hadn't carelessly left the tissue in a mess. It would have been completely out of character.

She told Rebecca what had happened after she entered the store.

"I'm certain I locked the counter and also the back door," Rebecca said. "I specifically remember locking both, just as always. I remember thinking about the garden tonight while locking up, and wishing it was summer again as I put the key into the lock."

Mary let out another anxious breath. "That's good to hear. I have a call into Chief McArthur, who will want to know if I'm certain the doors were locked, the case secured. I believe you."

They were still standing near the entrance when a young and pregnant Heidi Gilbert seemed to almost blow in on the wind. She wore a backpack instead of a purse, as young people often did, and her denim coat looked too thin. She'd wrapped a multicolored knitted scarf with a knotted and frayed fringe around her neck, so at least that provided some warmth.

As she stepped inside, the roar of a motorcycle seemed to almost disappear on the wind.

Mary smiled and welcomed her. Heidi had stopped by the shop soon after she and her husband moved to town. Mary had been drawn to the young woman immediately, perhaps because she seemed like a bit of a waif who needed protecting. Heidi didn't have a formal education, but she was curious about everything. She seemed quite taken with the children's nook and spent much time there, paging through the colorful picture books, perhaps dreaming about reading to the child she carried. She readily signed up for the Winter Warmth Book Chat even though she had admitted to Mary in a whisper, so other customers couldn't overhear, that she was a very slow reader.

Now as Heidi stood in front of her, her cheeks pink from the cold, Mary realized she must have looked as dismayed about Heidi's arrival on a motorcycle as she felt.

Heidi giggled. "If you're wondering about the noise, that was my husband Cade. He dropped me off."

Mary smiled as she tried to reserve judgment. "You are a brave soul to ride a motorcycle in your condition." She reached for Heidi's ice-cold hand and drew her farther into the warm bookshop. "The fireplace is going, the coffee and teakettle are on— Oh dear, can you have either?"

Heidi removed her knitted cap, unwound the neck scarf, and tossed back her dark hair. As she slipped her backpack from her shoulders, she laughed. "If you've got herbal tea, that'll work fine. Although a packet of cocoa mix would be even better. And marshmallows. For some reason, I've been craving marshmallows. Even if they're the little dried-up packaged ones, that's okay."

Mary gave the girl's icy hand a squeeze. "We've got both. Help yourself to anything you'd like."

Heidi smiled, pulled her jacket closer, and hurried to join the others.

The door opened again, and three more people entered: Sandra Rink, a teller at the Ivy Bay Bank & Trust, who gave Mary one of her endearing smiles, showing the tiny gap between her teeth; Clayton Strong, a middle-aged local contractor, wearing his usual ball cap; and Dorothy Johnson, a member of Mary's prayer group, who quickly shrugged out of a beautiful woolen cape with a natural-hued yarn fringe that seemed to dance when she moved. She wore a striking winter pantsuit, accessorized by a string of pearls on a mauve cashmere mock turtleneck. She smiled as Mary greeted her, but her eyes quickly darted around the room until she spotted Henry. He seemed to sense her stare and turned, smiled, and gave her a little wave.

Mary went over to the circle of folding chairs around the fireplace, mentally counting to see if they had enough seating. So far, the chat consisted of Rebecca, Bob Hiller, Henry Woodrow, Heidi Gilbert, Sandra Rink, Clayton Strong, Dorothy Johnson, and Betty. Rebecca's Great-aunt Millicent would join them later. Henry had made sure there was plenty of seating for all, leaving a few empty chairs for latecomers.

Coffee mugs and teacups in hand, the group milled back to the circle of chairs in front of the fireplace. Mary took her place near the fireplace, where she had a view of the front door in case anyone else arrived. It also provided her a view of the counter, where *The Murder of Roger Ackroyd* rested under lock and key.

The truth was, she felt jittery about all that had happened since the call from Rathburn. First, the amazing news about the sale, then to find the book tampered with, followed by the slamming back door and the thought that she might have interrupted a robbery in progress…and that she'd possibly been in the shop with the thief. All of it made her hands shake.

She placed her hands in her lap to hold them still and smiled at the others as they seated themselves.

And on top of her other concerns, she wanted everyone in the circle to be comfortable with the book chat and feel free to speak their minds. She especially didn't want to come across as the leader just because this was her shop. It was her hope that all would feel free to talk about their thoughts on the book.

She exchanged a glance with Henry, who was seated on the opposite side of the circle. He seemed to read her thoughts and gave her a wink and a smile. She breathed a little easier and smiled back.

She took a deep breath and said, "It's great to see all of you tonight. The winds are putting us all in need of some winter warmth, I suspect."

"I think it was a super idea," Heidi said, fingering a strand of her dark hair. "The days and weeks after Christmas can be such a letdown. Sad, somehow, if you don't have something to get out and do, or someplace to go."

"Cold, windy nights are meant for reading," Sandra Rink said. "I'm sure this won't be the first."

"Or the last," Clayton said.

The wind gusted, rattling the windows, and everyone chuckled. "Right on cue," Bob Hiller said, laughing. "This nor'easter is on its way for sure." He took a large bite of one of Betty's oatmeal cookies and leaned back contentedly. "I don't know which I like best, this great book or sitting around a friendly fireplace with all of you."

He quirked a brow. "Some of you might be surprised to hear me say that. You probably think of me only as your mail carrier." He finished his cookie, wiped his fingers on a paper napkin, and then flipped through his well-worn copy of *Murder on the Orient Express*. He grinned again. "But there's more to me than just a pretty face." He laughed heartily.

"I've recently started reading more than I have in a very long time."

He leaned forward, his shoulders hunched, and his expression turned solemn. "The truth is," he said, "I've had a lot on my mind, with my little granddaughter Isabella being so sick in the hospital and all. I've spent a lot of time on my days off, sitting with her mom and dad in the waiting room. Sometimes I'm there alone, waiting my turn to go in. I didn't think I'd be able to concentrate, but this Miss Christie, my goodness, she's a writer, all right. Kept me busy turning those pages. Helped me put aside my concerns about little Isabella for a while."

Bob turned to Mary. "But I didn't mean to get us off the topic of the book chat."

"That's okay, Bob. We're all concerned about Isabella," Mary said, the sadness in Bob's expression tugging at her heart. "Before we go on, why don't you tell us how she's doing?" Even as she spoke, she thought about how much she wanted to tell her news about the book and the help it would bring to the family.

"She's a little fighter, that girl." Tears filled his eyes. "She needs a kidney. I went in to volunteer, thinking because I'm a blood relative, I would be a good match, but the doctors say I'm too old. We need someone younger. They don't even need to be related. They have medicines now that make the nonblood-relative thing work.

"But they tell me her best chance is to go to Boston Children's Hospital where they do a lot of these. We've got her on a waiting list for a kidney there. And her mom and dad are working with the insurance company right now, trying to get approval."

He looked around the circle. "That's the rub. Insurance has run out. They reached the cap, and the insurance company is balking about moving her." His eyes filled again. He pulled out his handkerchief and blew his nose. "Sadly, the transplant costs more than you can imagine."

Mary had known some of this, had known that a medical charity organization had stepped in to see that Isabella had proper care in the local hospital. But they were still trying to get the funding to move her to Boston Children's. She glanced toward the front of the shop and drew in a deep breath as her gaze landed on the beautiful, leather-bound copy of *The Murder of Roger Ackroyd*. Made even more beautiful by what it now represented: a little girl's health.

"I'm sorry to go on," Bob said, hunched over again. "It's just so fresh in my mind. We all love that little girl so much—" His voice broke off.

"We care too," Mary said softly as the others murmured their own caring thoughts. "All of us do—for Isabella and your son and daughter-in-law. Please let us know if there's anything we can do for the family."

Bob blew his nose again. "For now, I could use another one or two of those oatmeal cookies. Then let's get this Orient Express back on the rails."

He got up and walked to the refreshment table. Henry went over with him, threw an arm around his shoulders, and then grabbed a few cookies of his own. Sandra and Clayton got up and refilled their drinks and then came back to sit down.

Sandra shot her special smile around the circle and then lifted her hand. "I have a few thoughts, if that's okay." She didn't wait for anyone's permission but forged ahead. "I loved the book. I mean, I wasn't sure what to expect, because, well, it's old-fashioned. I mean, Miss Christie wrote this, like, decades ago. It took me a while to get into her style, but after a few pages, I was drawn into the story like she'd grabbed me by the hand and yanked me onto that train herself."

Light laughter rose from around the circle.

"I mean, listen to this...." She thumbed through the book and stopped a few pages in. "Here, if I can make it out." She squinted and turned in her seat so the book's pages caught the amber light of the fire. "Here it is: 'He was a man of between sixty and seventy. From a little distance he had the bland aspect of a philanthropist. His slightly bald head, his domed forehead, the smiling mouth that displayed a very white set of false teeth, all seemed to speak of a benevolent personality. Only the eyes belied this assumption. They were small, deep set and crafty. Not only that. As the man, making some remark to his young companion, glanced across the room, his gaze stopped on Poirot for a moment, and just for that second there was a strange malevolence, and unnatural tensity in the glance.'"

Sandra looked up, her eyes bright. "Don't you just love that? I had to look up some of the words, but even before I did, I knew the meaning of what was going on. *Tensity.* I mean, it's a great word. You just know scary times are ahead, just from the 'unnatural tensity' in that glance."

A few members of the group contributed affirming words to Sandra for her observations, and Mary was encouraged by how it seemed people had really taken the book chat seriously.

"Anyone want to add a passage they particularly enjoyed, or perhaps a character?" Mary said after the conversation Sandra had started had died down.

Betty cleared her throat and spoke for a few minutes about the differences between Poirot, the sleuth in Agatha Christie's early novels, and Miss Marple, the sleuth in her later works.

Mary grinned at her sister. She had no idea that Betty had done such a comparison. She leaned forward. "And which do you like the best?"

Betty laughed. "Miss Marple. But I have to admit it's because of the British TV series I've seen with that actress… What's her name…?"

"Joan Hickson," Dorothy filled in, then looked around the circle, her gaze pausing briefly on Henry. "You know, don't you, Agatha Christie based Miss Marple on her grandmother? However, experts think the name came from a train station in Scotland that Miss Christie once passed through."

Betty chimed in. "Well, I liked Joan Hickson's portrayal of Miss Marple. She made her seem like such a gentle, wise soul."

"But smart as a whip," Henry added. "Just as all sleuths should be. We may not see them in action all the time—in real life, I mean—but I would wager, there are some minds in the real world that don't let many details pass them by when they're trying to puzzle a mystery."

Clayton looked down at the book in his lap, then around the circle. "Speaking of details, I think what I liked best about the story line was the fact that all the suspects were stuck in one place for the duration of the investigation."

"That's known as a closed crime," Dorothy said, her chin tilting upward. "Many say, in that regard alone, Christie has no equal."

Clayton didn't seem to notice her condescending tone, and went on. "Fourteen people are on the train when it gets stuck in a snowstorm traveling from Cairo to Calais. Hercule Poirot is an absolute genius as he works through the details to figure out the murderer." Clayton chuckled, thumping his copy of the book on his knee. "He's known to be an intellectual and a gentleman, so I didn't expect this dapper British guy to be so, well, human."

"Ah, that's not quite true," Dorothy said. "Anyone know why?" She raised a brow, obviously not expecting anyone to answer.

"He's Belgian, not English," Heidi said, grinning. "He's definitely smart. I don't think I could ever be so clever as to figure out who committed a crime like he did. But I liked him too, Mr. Strong. He almost became real to me." Mary was impressed. For a girl who claimed not to be very bookish, she seemed to have understood the text quite well.

"That's what sets gifted authors apart from the others," Dorothy said. "They bring characters to life, make them seem like someone who could live down the street from you. An author can make characters as intellectual, fun, or creepy as he or she wants."

Mary exchanged glances with Betty. Dorothy Johnson obviously wanted to take over the discussion by playing a professorial role. Mary wondered if she was trying to impress Henry, whom she'd been known to have set her sights on more than once.

No one else seemed to notice, so Mary sat back and listened.

"Creepy?" Heidi was saying. "That's why I like stories with happy endings and happy characters. If I see, er, read a book with a creepy character, I can't sleep at night. And"—she patted her belly—"that's when I get a lot of jumpy little legs and arms." She paused. "I love stories that aren't true...."

"Fiction, or novels," Dorothy filled in with a knowing sniff.

Heidi smiled. "It's fiction I like, then, I guess, but Cade—he's my husband—mostly reads mechanics magazines, especially if they're about motorcycles. He has a motorcycle he's been restoring for years. He's so proud of it his buttons almost burst. He works really hard, so I guess he can use his spare time as he chooses. I worry a little about how he'll handle things after the babies come, but he says I don't need to."

Betty sat forward. "Babies?"

Heidi grinned at the hubbub around the circle and patted her stomach again. "We're having twins. But it's going to be hard. We're still living with Cade's mom and dad—we just don't have a lot of money—but they don't really have room for the two of us, let alone a family of four."

Everyone seemed to be talking at once now, congratulating the young mother and asking questions about her due date. In the midst of it all, the front door opened and a wisp of a woman in her early eighties, not more than five feet tall, with snow-white curls and thick glasses, gingerly stepped in. She appeared almost too weak to stand, her right leg trembling as she leaned against her cane.

"Is this Mary's Bookshop?" Without waiting for an answer, she closed the door behind her, cheeks rosy from the cold, glasses fogging from the bookshop's warmth.

"Aunt Millicent!" Rebecca cried. "You made it."

"I did, indeed, though it's a wonder." Millicent folded her collapsible cane and held out her arms as Rebecca raced over to give her a hug. "It's quite a storm out there. The roads were a mess of downed branches."

"Please come in and get warm," Rebecca said.

"Actually, I can't. I'm waiting for someone." Millicent turned back to the front window and peered out. "I brought someone with me. He's out parking his car."

Rebecca looked alarmed. "You brought a . . . a man with you?"

"Oh goodness, no," Millicent said, looking stricken. "It's not what you think. There was this man standing outside the shop just now, and I asked if I could help him. He said his GPS is malfunctioning. He asked me for directions to an address on the bay. I said that I had no idea where anything is in this town, but I knew some people who probably do." She glanced around the room. "I hope that's okay." Her laugh was musical and contagious.

Mary went over to her and put her arm around Millicent's shoulders. "You did exactly the right thing. Of course, we'll help him. This is no night to be lost." Outside, the wind had picked up again, and in the distance, it sounded like the rain might have started.

The lights flickered, then came back on before anyone could do anything more than gasp. A second later, the front door opened again. As the bell jingled, a handsome middle-aged man in a dark topcoat stepped through the doorway. Holding an expensive-looking briefcase, he looked like he'd just stepped out of Bloomingdale's in New York City. He nodded pleasantly, but Mary noticed that though his mouth tilted upward into a smile, the rest of his face was filled with tension.

"This is quite the welcoming party," he said easily. "This young lady"—he glanced at Millicent—"tells me that you're just the folks who can help a stranger in need."

Before anyone could speak, he glanced down at the book Mary still held in her hands. His expression changed. "Well, look at that. *Murder on the Orient Express.* One of my favorites." His gaze then took in the others who were holding copies of the same book. "Don't tell me I've stumbled into a meeting of the local Agatha Christie fan club." His smile widened. "I'm quite a fan myself."

"Come in out of the cold," Bob Hiller said, his tone friendly and authoritative. If anyone could help the man with directions, it was Bob, who, because of his mail route, knew Ivy Bay's roads like the back of his hand. "What can we help you with?"

Mary moved back to the circle of chairs, assuming the newcomers were right behind her.

The wind suddenly took on the sound of a distant freight train, growing louder as it neared.

"Oh dear," Heidi gasped, grabbing her belly.

"My goodness," Dorothy said, sounding displeased. Others let out murmurs of alarm. Mary and Betty shared a startled look just before the power went off.

All Mary could think about was *The Murder of Roger Ackroyd* in the case near the door and her purse right next to it.

The lights were out, and the last glance she had of the stranger placed him near both.

FOUR

L et's remain calm, everyone," Henry said warmly, staring at his cell phone. "This may only last a few minutes. Meanwhile, I'll turn up the gas logs and see if we can get more light." He paused and then said, "Strange, it seems to be getting dimmer."

Mary sighed. "It's vented, so it needs electricity to run."

Henry harrumphed while he still fiddled with his cell. "No bars. The towers must be down." Mary's cell was in her purse behind the counter, but from the look of things—which was quickly fading as the fireplace continued to dim—the only other person in the group who had a cell phone in hand was Clayton, and he didn't seem to be able to connect either. Henry put his cell in his pocket. "Do you have anything we can use for light? Flashlights, lanterns, candles?"

Mary took comfort in Henry's voice. She suspected he'd spoken up for her sake, knowing how worried she would be over the book. She tried to remember where she'd last placed the flashlight. And heaven only knew where there might be a lantern. Candles? She sighed, thinking she might have seen some in a box in the back room.

Flashlight. She knew they had one, but where was it? As if reading her mind, Rebecca spoke up. "I think I used the flashlight last and left it in one of the drawers in the back room."

"Great," Mary said. "Do you think you can make your way there in the dark?"

"I can try."

"Also, I believe we have some other items we can use. Henry, would you mind going down to the cellar? I think there might be an old kerosene lamp down there, and if we're in luck, maybe some fuel for it." She chuckled. "And with even better luck, an intact wick."

Henry said he'd be happy to and opened his cell phone again, which provided a very soft glow.

"Thanks," Rebecca said, from a few steps away. "I'm not the most graceful person God ever created, and in the dark...well, who knows what could happen." She chuckled and quickly stepped into the dim beam of Henry's cell. They both followed its bouncing glow to the back room. He stayed with Rebecca long enough for her to find the flashlight with a loud "Aha!" Then Mary heard his heavy shoes clomping down the basement stairs.

"I'm also checking for matches and whatever else I can find," Rebecca called to the others.

A general hubbub filled the shop as people discussed their dilemma, whether the storm was local, whether to go home or to stay put.

"How about candles?" Bob Hiller called to Rebecca.

"Are there any left over from the Christmas display— maybe the Advent wreath?" Mary considered out loud to Rebecca.

"No, I think we used all of those," Rebecca called back. "But there might be another flashlight. Bob, can you come help me look?"

Bob made his way to the back room.

Mary spoke up, keeping her voice calm. "Let's settle in until we know more about what's going on. We'll make a call to the police station, once we get reception, and find out what we can about the blackout, how widespread, if it's safe to be on the roads."

"I'm not sure...." Betty sounded worried. "Maybe we should all return to our homes."

"I know what it's like out there, and I don't think it's safe to leave." Mary recognized the speaker as Millicent, whose voice shook. She sounded frightened. "It's terrible. I almost didn't make it."

Either out of curiosity or disagreement, a few shadowy figures headed to the front of the shop, presumably to look out the large window.

"Listen!" someone exclaimed. "It's rain. Hard rain."

"Cats and dogs," someone else said.

Henry came back in, and the basement door banged shut behind him. He chuckled as he walked toward the group, his cell phone leading the way. "The good news is, I found the old kerosene lamp and a can of kerosene."

"And the bad news?" Dorothy asked, almost sounding hopeful. Mary wondered if she wanted Henry to come to the rescue with something a bit magical.

"The wick is in pretty bad shape," he said. "It's quite old, almost to the point of disintegrating before my eyes. But I think I can make it work."

"Wonderful!" Dorothy said.

Bob cleared his throat as he came back, rattling another flashlight that wasn't working. "I heard somebody say they were thinking of leaving. I think the worst thing we could do is get back on the roads, don't you think, Clayton? You know those roads as well as anyone. That last blast was a doozy, and now it's raining to beat the band." Clayton knew the roads almost as well as Bob, with his work as a contractor.

"I agree," Clayton said.

Mary's eyes were adjusting to the ambient light from Rebecca's flashlight in the back room, and after a few minutes, she could make out Henry bending over the antique lamp, which he'd placed on the refreshment table. Bob went over to help him.

"I'm quite certain everything is fine," Dorothy said with an air of finality, as if her saying it made it so. "I think someone needs to take charge. I say we disband and try this again next week. You did say, didn't you, Mary, that it was to be a rather informal get-together? It can't get much more informal than this." She laughed. "I, for one, am ready for home and hearth."

At her words, a few more people moved to the front door, disappearing into the darkest corner of the shop—the place where Mary had last seen the stranger, the man who'd entered the shop just as the lights went out. Another loud blast of wind, this time accompanied by rain, sliced into the windows. She heard a few gasps.

A man's chuckle. It wasn't Bob's, Henry's, or Clayton's.

Rustling sounds, people moving, the faint jingle of a key in someone's pocket or handbag, followed by more footsteps.

Mary breathed a prayer that she could remain calm in the midst of the worrisome chatter and milling.

Taking a deep breath, she again turned her attention to the book in the glass case, her purse behind the counter near the cash register, and the shop still too dark to see who was where. Or the stranger she'd last seen standing by the door.

She made her way toward the front of the shop. Behind her, she could hear Clayton putting in his good-natured two cents about how to get the wick to work on the antique lamp.

The closer Mary moved to the counter, the more certain she was that someone, or maybe more than one person, was standing behind it.

She spoke with forced cheerfulness. "Whoever's drifted in this direction, I invite you to come back to our chairs until Bob and Henry can light the lamp. As soon as our eyes get used to the old-fashioned lamplight, we can continue on with our book chat." She laughed lightly to calm any nerves that might be frazzled, and as the wind continued howling, she sensed there were many. "And, don't forget, the refreshment table is nearby. I'm sure there'll soon be enough light to find Betty's cookies."

"Refreshments?" The unfamiliar voice was that of the stranger. Near the cash register. "If I had to stumble accidentally into a shop when the lights went out," he went on, "I certainly picked the right place." He laughed again, but there was a tightness to his tone.

Mary continued to move toward him, her thoughts on the book—not his compliment.

"Please, come and join us," Dorothy said, suddenly at Mary's elbow. They were within a few feet of a shadowy figure. "I heard you mention that you're an Agatha Christie fan," Dorothy continued.

Mary bit her tongue. No, she actually wasn't comfortable with this stranger in her shop, standing too near the valuable book. Besides, there was something sinister about the way this fellow had blown in just before the lights went out.

"Don't you agree?" Dorothy went on pleasantly.

"Agree...?" Mary managed.

"That this Agatha Christie fan should stay for the book chat."

Mary forced herself to think of the number of Scripture verses about entertaining strangers in your midst. And he was definitely that. With a whispered prayer, she swallowed hard. "Yes, of course," she said.

"I can't see a thing," the man said, "though it seems I've encountered a cat. At least something that's furry and purrs." As he spoke, his voice dropped and he grunted softly as he apparently stooped to pick up Gus. "There, there, big guy," he said. "You'll be better off up here."

"Up here?" Mary said, alarmed. "Up where?"

"I just placed the cat on the counter so I wouldn't trip over it. I have no idea how to navigate my way over to where the rest of you are."

"Here, I'll show you," Sandra said, surprising Mary that she was so near.

"Don't forget me," Millicent said weakly. Another surprise. She assumed Millicent had gone back to the circle with Rebecca. "I suffer from night blindness. Could someone help me?"

Mary followed the sound of Millicent's voice and within a few seconds had her arm around the older woman, who was trembling more than before, and now used her cane. "I don't know how you're holding up so well," Mary said to encourage her. "After the long drive, now this..."

"I'm ready to sit down, that's for sure," Millicent said, letting Mary support her on one side, using the cane on the other, as they made their way back to the chairs.

Henry and Clayton shared a shout of triumph as the antique lamp came to life. Henry held it up triumphantly, searched for Mary, and when he met her eyes, he grinned. "This will add a festive air to our chat. I, for one, look forward to getting beyond the storm's interruption and back to Agatha Christie."

Mary smiled her thanks, knowing Henry had said it loud enough for everyone to hear, and she swept her gaze through the shop, ending back at the glass counter. Gus was now asleep atop the counter near the cash register. Beneath him, the cardboard box was where she'd left it, and it appeared undisturbed.

A few folks helped themselves to hot drinks, and Betty passed around a plate of cookies. Everyone then settled into their chairs once more. Outside, the rain came down in sheets, and the wind kept up its blasting gusts.

"Thank you for your hospitality," the stranger said. "My name's Nigel Finnian, and I'm new to town. I had hoped to get settled in before this nor'easter hit...." He shrugged. "But thanks for inviting me to join you."

As others introduced themselves, Nigel seemed nervous. Understandable, Mary supposed, trying to give him the benefit of the doubt. They were all anxious because of the storm.

Henry handed Nigel his copy of the book. "Like I said," Nigel continued, "this is one of my favorites of Christie's. I've loved to read since I was a young boy, but Agatha Christie soon became a favorite—after I'd finished reading everything by Edgar Allan Poe, of course."

Mary watched his face in the flickering light of the kerosene lamp. His features didn't quite match the lighthearted banter about his reading habits. And his monologue seemed like a nervous cover-up for something he wasn't saying.

She held back a shiver, wondering what the real reason was that he'd stopped at the bookshop. Then again, the dark and stormy setting probably was making her paranoid.

She glanced at the counter again. Now that the lamp cast a glow across the room, she could better make out the details. Gus slept peacefully on the countertop, oblivious to the rain and wind.

"Let's get back to the *Orient Express*, shall we?" Dorothy pointedly looked at her watch.

"A good idea," Mary said pleasantly. "Why don't you start?"

Dorothy beamed, now that she had center stage. "Agatha Christie, of course, has quite a history herself. Parts of her life read better than any of her fictional mysteries. In my opinion, anyway." She glanced at Henry, and her lips curved into a smile. "*Murder on the Orient Express*, as I said earlier, shows her writing as unique to the time period, the idea especially of a 'closed mystery,' and, I believe, she was the first to..."

She was still going on and on with detail—which Mary suspected she'd gleaned from Wikipedia—when out of the corner of her eye, Mary noticed Heidi was attempting to stifle a yawn and Bob's eyelids were drooping. Eventually, Dorothy quieted, as the room had done long before her.

Mary broke in gently. "Thank you so much, Dorothy. Does anyone else want to chime in with their thoughts?"

Heidi Gilbert locked eyes with Mary for a moment, then seemed to reconsider and put her head down.

"Heidi? Any last thoughts?" Mary nudged, not wanting anyone to be steamrollered by Dorothy's monologue.

Heidi's head was still down, and a short moment later, obviously aware that all eyes were on her, she looked up. "It's just...well, I waited all night for the right time to tell you all something, and I guess there's no time like the present...." She sniffled. "I have a...a confession to make." She pulled a tissue from her backpack. "It's about the book...."

Before she could finish, the lights flickered once, twice, then came back on to stay.

FIVE

———◆◆◆———

"You were about to tell us something," Mary said after she'd approached Heidi, who was still seated, while the rest of the group had begun to mill about and share celebratory conversation with the lights back on.

The young woman flushed and fluttered her hand. "It wasn't important. Really."

Mary saw something in Heidi's expression that caught her attention. Was it guilt? Her mind flew back to the book in the case, the tampering someone had done with the intent of taking it. She searched Heidi's troubled eyes, but it was obvious the moment had passed when she said she needed to "confess."

Henry had flipped open his phone. "Aha. Four bars," he said. "I think we're in business to try the police again." He punched in some numbers. "It's ringing." He spoke in low tones for a few minutes, and then he flipped his phone closed. "Branches were down on a tower and power line, but it's now cleared. He did say that we should be aware of downed branches on the roads, though. Also said a heavier band of rain is about an hour offshore." He looked at Mary. "The deputy's advice is for us to head for home before it hits. Oh, and, Mary, the chief wants to speak with you." He handed his phone to Mary.

Mary stepped away from the others, and when Chief McArthur came on the line, she explained what had happened since Orris Rathburn's call.

"It's worth how much?" The police chief sounded incredulous.

Mary repeated the number, and the chief let out a low whistle. "No wonder you're worried. Tell you what, leave everything as is so I can take a look. The packaging you say was tampered with. The works. I'll stop by in about a half hour. After that, my suggestion is that you take the book home with you for the night. Maybe the courier could pick it up there."

Mary ended the call, feeling better now that the chief was involved.

Mary cleared her throat. "Thanks, everyone, for coming out tonight. Despite the interruption, I think we had a terrific conversation, and I'm really pleased that you were all here to discuss the book, as sorry as I am for the power outage.

"Though we hadn't planned for this to be a formal, regular meeting kind of book club, because of tonight's storm we'll meet same place, same time next week."

"With electricity," someone said and chuckled. Others joined in the laughter.

The group began to put on their coats and hunt for their keys. Nigel gathered his topcoat and briefcase from a nearby chair. "Thank you for letting me join you for these very interesting few minutes. I never expected to find an Agatha Christie book club when I followed this little lady to your shop." He smiled at

Millicent, who looked up and gave him a nod. "Now, if someone would kindly tell me how to find my address, I'll be on my way." He shook his head slowly. "It has been quite a while since I've been here, but I didn't think I'd have this much trouble."

Henry took Nigel's card, read the handwritten address on the back, and then gave him directions, with Bob Hiller filling in details.

Dorothy stepped up. "We're glad you stopped in," she said, as if she was responsible for the evening.

Mary walked with them to the door. Nigel seemed to walk in lockstep with her, blocking her view of the counter to their left. Was he doing this on purpose? She didn't want to come to any rash decisions before she knew that the book was safe, but on the other hand, what if it had been taken during the blackout?

With another thank-you for the cookies and coffee, Nigel turned to Mary. "I may be in Ivy Bay for some time. Would you mind if I join you and the others for the next chat?"

Mary swallowed hard, unsure she liked the idea. There was something troubling about him.

Before she could answer, Dorothy said, "Yes, of course." The others gathered their books and coats. Heidi grabbed her backpack, and Millicent picked up her yarn tote and cane, while Rebecca helped Betty put away the refreshments.

Millicent seemed to sense Mary's gaze and looked up. Her eyes were red-rimmed, something Mary hadn't noticed earlier. She went over to see if she could help her with her coat. Her tremor was more noticeable now, and Mary's heart went out to her. Fatigue seemed to be setting in quickly. "I'm glad you could join us tonight."

"Me too," she said. "When Rebecca asked me to come for a visit, I couldn't say no. I had a million and one things I thought I needed to attend to, but it turns out, this was where I needed to be. I enjoyed meeting everyone."

She pulled a tissue from her sleeve. "It hits me in waves sometimes. I'll be fine, and then I remember something about Oliver, an expression, a word, something I think I'd like to call and tell him about...like tonight. For just an instant, I thought about calling him to tell him I made it safely through the storm. Then I remembered...I couldn't." She lowered her head and blew her nose. "We were married for over sixty years, you know."

Mary put her arm around the grieving woman. "I understand. I've been through it too." She paused as the image of John's smile filled her heart. "I'm still going through it."

Millicent nodded. "Thank you. Sometimes I feel like such a crybaby, like I should be stronger than I am. I've always thought that I'm as brave as an old oak tree, but in reality, I feel I could topple over at any time."

"Tears are meant to help us heal," Mary said. "I think God gave us tears for that reason."

Rebecca came up and took her great-aunt's arm and walked her toward the door. "Where's Heidi?" Rebecca glanced around the room. "I wanted to find out what she was about to tell us when the lights came back on."

"I asked her about it, but she seemed reluctant to say. I didn't see her leave," Mary said. "She must have slipped out with the others."

When it seemed the shop was empty, Mary and Betty headed to the refreshment table to finish cleaning up. They chatted as they carried things into the back room. Someone or some people—Mary suspected it was the three men—had folded the chairs and carried them into the cellar. After a few minutes, she was ready to lock up.

Just as she turned out the light in the back room, Mary heard a shuffling noise in the front of the shop. She shot a warning glance at Betty who was a few feet behind her, and they both halted midstep. As Mary put her finger to her lips, one thought chilled her. She hadn't locked the door after the guests left.

Anyone could have slipped in.

"Who's there?" Mary called out.

"It's just me," Heidi said, stepping out of the shadows, her knitted cap and fringed scarf in place. "I started to leave with the others, then realized I couldn't until Cade gets here. I don't know where he is. He's always on time."

"Surely he's not coming on the motorcycle again?" Betty asked, not hiding her concern, which matched Mary's.

Heidi shrugged. "I'm used to it. And he's a good driver." She lifted her chin a notch. "I hope it's okay to sit here and watch for him." She nodded toward the stool behind the counter. "It's too cold and rainy to wait outside."

Mary couldn't help glancing at the box in the glass case. It appeared undisturbed. "Of course. But why don't you give him a call? I'll drive you home. I'm happy to do it." Not only would the young woman be safer and warmer, it would give Mary a chance to find out what she was about to confess earlier.

"Really?" Heidi said, her face lighting up. "I would like that."

"Would you like to call him? You can use my phone."

Heidi nodded. "Thank you. I—we—don't have cell phones."

While Heidi made the call, Mary grabbed her purse and double-checked that the glass case that held her rare books was locked. It was secure.

"I'll take Gus home," Betty said as Mary slung her purse over one shoulder and picked up the carrier in her other hand.

"Good idea. I need to stop by to meet Chief McArthur, anyway. Poor Gus has already had a long day."

Heidi was still whispering into the phone when Mary hurried to Betty's car with Gus. She placed the carrier in the backseat, opened the driver's door for Betty, who was right behind her and quickly slid behind the steering wheel.

Mary gestured to Heidi to join her, and the young woman flipped the phone closed and hurried through the door to the Impala. As Mary trotted back to the shop to lock up, splats of rain were just beginning to fall again.

She waved to Betty as she pulled out and turned the opposite direction. The wind had died down, but she remembered the warning Henry had relayed about a second band of rain offshore and turned to Heidi. She needed to get back as quickly as possible to avoid keeping the chief waiting.

"Is your home far?" During her visits to the shop, Heidi hadn't mentioned where she lived—only that it was with her in-laws.

Heidi gave Mary the directions. "It's a short ride." She grinned. "Of course, that's on the Harley."

They rode in silence for a few minutes, then Mary looked across to Heidi. "You were about to tell us something tonight…a confession, you said. Is it important? I mean, is there something you want to talk about?" Her words were spoken gently, but fear squeezed her heart. What if this young pregnant woman was the one who'd tampered with the book? What would she do? She tried to relax. In the end, no one had actually taken the book, and that's what mattered.

Heidi looked over at Mary and sighed deeply. "Well, I wasn't going to say anything, because, really, I'm pretty embarrassed about it. But after the TV movies were brought up, I guess I felt I should confess about how I 'read' this book." At the word *read*, she used air quotes.

"Read?" Mary let out a sigh of her own, a relieved sigh. "I remember that you said you don't read very fast."

"It's not just that. I can't read very well at all. So I rented the DVD and watched *Murder on the Orient Express* on TV so I'd know what to talk about."

She paused. "I heard Cade's ma and pa talking to each other about how sad it was that Cade married somebody like me, that I'll never amount to much. And that's without them knowing the trouble I have, how I get words mixed up and turned around. They only know that I dropped out of school to marry their son and then right off the bat, got pregnant." She lifted her chin almost defiantly. "One of the reasons I signed up for the book chat was so I could prove to Cade's family that I'm smarter than they think I am. They think I'm reading the book."

Mary's heart went out to Heidi. "That's a pretty heavy burden to carry." As heavy as the twins she was expecting.

Heidi nodded. "I was going to tell everyone tonight that I'd watched the movie. But after the lights went on, I was too scared to. I don't think I should carry on the lie, though. I don't think I can come back. Those people are all so nice; it doesn't seem right."

"I don't think you should quit. Not at all." She turned down Heidi's street and slowed the car as they approached a double-wide trailer attached to a carport. The land around it was bleak. Mary's headlights hit upon a beat-up washing machine at one end of the carport and a workbench with various engine parts along the side. A decades-old car with flat tires sat wet and forlorn outside the carport.

"This is it," Heidi said.

"I would love for you to tell us all about the film. Pay close attention to the scenes and the characters. It will be a great comparison."

"Really?" She reached for the door handle as she looked at Mary, her eyes luminous with tears.

"Please." There was such raw hope in her expression that Mary had to swallow the sting at the back of her throat. "You don't need to say anything about reading. As far as the others are concerned, you agreed to do this comparison because I asked you to."

"I could even tell Cade's mom and dad that you asked me to do it. That way I don't have to sneak around and watch the DVD when no one else is home." She grinned and swiped at her tears. "It could be like I'm taking a class in school or something." She reached for her backpack.

"You're welcome to stop by the shop anytime you want. I'll find some books that you could take your time with, and fall in love with."

Someone flipped the porch light on from inside, and a curtain opened a few inches.

"Thank you, Mrs. Fisher. For everything."

"You're quite welcome. We'll see you next time, then?"

Heidi grinned. "Sounds great."

"Or sooner, if you like. You're welcome at the shop anytime."

She shrugged, suddenly looking wary as the front door of the trailer opened and a woman looked out. "Maybe."

It struck Mary as odd that Cade's motorcycle was nowhere to be seen on the property.

Mary parked in front of the shop, and within seconds, Chief McArthur pulled up next to her in his cruiser. His six-foot frame seemed to almost unfold as he got out. He grinned at Mary as she opened her door. It warmed her heart to see this man she'd known since childhood.

"I know how busy you are," she said as they walked to the front door. She put the key in the lock and turned it. "I really appreciate you stopping by. Especially since this really isn't an emergency."

"I happened to be in the neighborhood," he said. "And anyway, if someone tried to take the book and failed, they might be back."

She opened the door, but Chief McArthur stopped her from entering first. "Let me," he said, then added with a half smile, "this is a case when chivalry means entering first to make sure everything's okay."

As soon as she was inside, Mary flipped on the lights. She let out a sigh. All seemed well.

"This is the case that was tampered with?" The chief went at once to the glass case. He squatted down to take a look. "Is it locked?" He pulled on a pair of silicone gloves.

Mary nodded. "Yes. It's been locked all evening. Plus, I checked it just before we left a little while ago."

He reached for the handle. "Good. It's still secure."

Mary handed him the key to the cabinet, he worked the lock, then handed it back.

"The book is in this box?"

She started to reach for it. "Let me," he said and reached into the case. As he lifted the box, his expression registered that it was lighter than he expected.

No. A whirl of emotions filled her. And questions. Who? When? Why? And again, Bob Hiller's precious granddaughter Isabella took precedence over all other thoughts. And her parents, their great need.

And the sale of the book that would make all the difference in the world.

"It's empty," he said, turning toward her.

Mary's heart dropped.

SIX

———◆◆◆———

Outside, the rain poured down, though not as heavy as earlier in the evening. A gust of wind blew down Main Street, and the Mary's Mystery Bookshop sign rattled against its iron post.

Mary watched as Chief McArthur, his forensic gloves still on, opened the box they both already knew was empty. The tissue paper she'd so carefully covered the book with, was still in place. Whoever took the book simply slipped it out without disturbing the wrapping and replaced the lid on the box.

The chief frowned and looked up at Mary. "Did you check the box before you left?"

"Only the counter to see if it was locked. And it was, so I assumed the book was in the box, just as I'd left it."

"How long were you gone?"

She told him about driving Heidi home. "Only fifteen minutes at the most."

"If someone knew what to look for and where, it could have been done in that time frame."

Mary nodded. "But they would have needed a key—to the case. I have mine with me."

"Was there any way someone could have gotten your key—earlier, I mean? Where do you usually keep it?"

"In my purse, which was in the cupboard next to you. There, under the cash register."

He glanced at the cupboard. "Do you keep it locked?"

Her heart sinking farther toward the floor, she shook her head. "There's really never been a need. Even tonight, I didn't think of it. I trusted the people who were here. It wasn't until later that a stranger joined us."

Chief McArthur frowned. "A stranger?" He pulled a spiral notepad and nubby pencil from his pocket. "Tell me about him or her."

She nodded. "A man came in asking for directions to a place on the bay."

"His name?"

"Nigel Finnian. Tall, dark hair, middle-aged."

"And you think he could have come around the counter without anyone seeing him?"

"It was quite dark at this end of the room, but...yes."

"The keys are in your purse, just as you left them?"

Mary checked. "Yes. In the outside zipper pocket. To find them—especially that quickly, someone would have needed to know where I keep them." She thought for a moment. "The cupboard door is tight. I think I would have heard it snap open and close again—I'm familiar with the sound. Very distinct."

"Though the rain and wind might have prevented that," he pointed out. He paused for a moment, absently tapping the pencil on the counter. "And I wonder how many women keep their keys in an outside pocket. Most, I suspect." He smiled. "I know my wife does." He looked over at the cupboard. "And that's a pretty convenient—and obvious—place to stash your purse, if you ask me."

Mary sighed heavily. "So you think anyone could have figured it out if they tried."

He shrugged and gave her a sheepish smile. "I hate to say so, but yes."

Mary sighed. "I guess I need to rethink where I put things." She pushed up her eyeglasses as reality sank in. "So it had to be someone who was here tonight," she said, feeling ready to jump out of her skin. This entire episode—from the elation of the news from Orris Rathburn to now—was almost too much to take in. "When the lights went out, there was confusion. People were moving here and there, some looking for emergency lighting, others trying to decide whether to leave or stay. Some came over here; others remained near where we were seated." She remembered Heidi sitting on the stool behind the counter as she waited for her husband to pick her up. The others who'd crowded to the door when the lights went out—Nigel, Millicent, Sandra, Dorothy and maybe Heidi too.

Chief McArthur narrowed his eyes in thought. "Let me have the names of those you think might have been near the case during that time. Also the names of everyone here tonight."

She didn't want to think of most of them as suspects, but she named them anyway.

"You'll need to provide information for a police report." The chief wrote a few things down on a pad. "Let me take a look around—and maybe you should too. See if anything else was taken, and also if the book might have been taken from the case and placed elsewhere in the store."

A long shot, but Mary was willing to try.

Mary closely examined her collection of rare books, the bookshelves, and even the children's nook. She found nothing out of place, nothing else missing. While Chief McArthur checked the back door for signs of forced entry and headed into the cellar to have a look around, Mary checked again behind the front counter. She knelt to inspect the floor.

A glint of silver caught her eye, and she bent lower to have a better look. On the floor on the far side of the cash register lay a comb—a man's comb with a thin silver frame across the back. It appeared to have the letters *RH* or *RW* in the center of a classical, ornate swirl, but the engraved letters were faded.

Then she saw a strand of yarn and some paper. The paper appeared to have been torn from a notebook planner of some sort. A few letters showed: *N U A R Y*, though no date. There were a few numbers written under it, but not enough to make sense of them. "Chief?" she called as he turned out the storeroom light. "Come take a look at this."

"Sharp eyes," he said, grinning, when he reached her. He picked up the comb and held it to the light.

"Do you see initials? Or writing of some sort?"

He brought it closer to his eyes. "Yes, yes…I see *RH*, or maybe *RW*. Very worn; so hard to tell." He started to drop it into a small plastic bag. "This may give us something. Good job."

Mary pulled out her phone. "Mind if I snap a picture before you take it?"

"Good thinking," the chief said. "If anything comes to you about its design, let me know."

She took shots from three different angles, and then he dropped it into the bag.

"Anything else?"

"A strand of yarn, which I'm sure is from Gus's toy mouse, and a tuft of cat hair, which is definitely his." They both smiled.

"There's one more interesting item." She gave him the scrap of paper she'd found on the floor near the cash register. "It appears to be the corner of a calendar page, maybe a planner."

"Letters $N U A R Y$, January," he guessed.

Mary nodded. "There's a number below, but it's torn in half. Could be a phone number or address."

"Do you recognize the handwriting?"

"No. It's not Rebecca's . . . or anyone else's that I recognize." She pulled out her phone again. "Mind if I take another picture?"

"No, go right ahead."

While she took a few shots, the chief examined the comb again, this time peering through the clear forensics bag. "None of this means anything to you?"

She shook her head.

His expression sobered. "I'm so sorry about this, Mary. I hope we can find the thief."

"Thank you, Chief," she said. "I'll be here tomorrow, if you need to send someone over to follow up." Though with the storm and the havoc it had caused, she figured they were stretched thin.

He made another note. "I'll have someone call—not sure who's on duty tomorrow or even if they can come. I'll check the duty roster and do my best. Though it may be later in the day." He hesitated. "With all that's going on—the accidents after the storm and such...."

"I understand."

With a heavy heart, Mary followed Chief McArthur out of the shop. He waited while she locked the door and had gotten into the Impala. Then he climbed into the cruiser and drove off.

Mary dialed Betty even before she pulled onto Main Street, even though their home was only minutes away, and told her briefly what had happened. It helped just to hear her sister's voice.

"Are you okay?"

"Just dismayed," Mary admitted. "And blaming myself for not being more careful. I shouldn't have left. Maybe someone slipped in—or stayed and hid after the chat—and took the book while I was gone."

"Hold that thought," Betty said. "I'm putting on the teakettle. Let's talk this through when you get home. The last thing you need to do is blame yourself."

"Always the big sister." Mary laughed lightly. "Thanks, Bets. I needed to hear that."

"I think I see your headlights. I'm off to pour that tea."

"I'm in here," Betty called when Mary walked in the door.

Mary stuck her head around the corner of the entryway and smiled. Betty waited in the living room, a pot of herbal tea and two floral teacups on the coffee table. Nearby, a small plate of cookies sat next to a stack of bright, colorful napkins.

Just what Mary needed on this dreary night: a chance to relax and get Betty's opinion on the theft, feel the warmth of the room, and gather her thoughts about the steps she needed to take next.

As she walked in to sit down beside Betty, she thought about God's greatest gifts in her life—her sister was at the top of the list, and of course, her friendship with Henry and others in town. It helped in times like these to think of her blessings even as she puzzled through troubling events.

Betty poured a cup of tea, placed it in the matching saucer, and handed it to Mary. "Now, where were we?" She lifted an eyebrow. "I think I'd just said something about not blaming yourself for what happened tonight."

Mary breathed in the faint fragrance of jasmine. "*Mmm*, just what I needed. Thank you. How did you know?"

Betty laughed and sat down next to Mary on the sofa. "After the blustery business indoors and out tonight, I'd already figured we both could use some tea and comfort. When I heard the distress in your voice, I was sure of it." She took a sip of her tea, studying Mary over the rim of her cup. Her expression turned somber. "You look like you need more comfort than tea." She leaned forward, her face lined with worry. Then she added, "You couldn't have prevented the theft. Someone obviously has had his or her eye on that book."

"I just can't figure out why," Mary said. "Or how he or she knew its value."

Betty studied her for a moment. "Could it have been taken for any other reason? Maybe the original owner had second thoughts, knew where it was, and wanted it back?"

"I wondered about that earlier." Mary narrowed her eyes in thought. "Tomorrow, I'll look into it. I know word can spread, but this fast?" She almost laughed at the ironic thought. "Not at such lightning speed, even in Ivy Bay." She paused, considering the idea again. It made sense that someone might have cleaned out their garage, let it go for nothing with a box of other books or odds and ends, heard about the $31,000 sale...But news simply couldn't have traveled that fast. Especially since she hadn't told anyone except Betty, Henry, and Chief McArthur, people she trusted implicitly.

Mary told Betty about meeting Chief McArthur at the bookshop and the items they'd discovered.

Betty shook her head slowly. "Do you think they might help lead to whoever did it?"

"I'm not sure." She sat forward. "But I plan to get started looking into the possibility first thing in the morning."

For a moment, the only sound in the room was the crackle of the fire. Gus came around the corner, spotted Mary, and hopped on the sofa and then curled in her lap, purring softly.

She took a sip of tea and closed her eyes for a moment, thinking about the people who were in attendance at the book chat. "I just can't imagine who would have done this." She opened her eyes, took off her glasses, and leaned forward. "Especially who. Think of those who were in the shop tonight. Of course, we might think of Nigel first. He's a stranger, was near the counter, and had access." She sighed and sat back. "But no key."

"Could he have gotten it from your purse?"

"According to the chief, I keep my keys in a similar pocket many women keep them in, his wife included." She shrugged.

"Same news about the cupboard being a pretty obvious place to put my purse. So it's entirely possible."

Betty leaned back against the sofa, frowning in thought. "What about Heidi? Could she have taken it? She was by the counter when you and I were putting away the refreshments. She was so quiet we didn't even know she was there."

Mary nodded. "Heidi may be a suspect. I found a piece of yarn when the chief was there, which I assumed was from one of Gus's toys, but she was wearing a tattered, knitted neck scarf, so the yarn could easily be a match. And you're right. She was certainly in the right place at the right time."

Mary nibbled her cookie, then took a sip of tea. She remembered how Heidi abruptly ended their conversation when the woman came to the door of the trailer and looked out. Did that mean anything? And the obvious circumstances she lived in, evident even in the dark. But how would she have known about the book to steal it?

"Who else, then?"

"Well, we don't know much about Rebecca's Aunt Millicent. She's never mentioned her before tonight when she said her aunt was on her way."

Betty stared at the fire for a moment and then turned back to Mary. "I thought it was strange that she came in with Nigel, didn't you?"

"That could have been the coincidence they said it was." Mary placed her teacup and saucer back on the coffee table. Then she chuckled. "Or not." She stood to walk over and stand by the fire. "She's still grieving over her late husband, is rather feeble, and she didn't arrive until tonight—so she couldn't have been the one who broke in earlier only to run off when she saw me coming."

Mary clasped her hands behind her, relishing the warmth of the fire seep into her fingers. "Besides, when something like this happens, does it necessarily have to be a stranger?" She yawned, suddenly feeling every bit of the weight of the day and all that had happened.

Betty gave Mary a gentle smile. "It's late. Why don't we sleep on all this? Things will seem better in the morning."

Mary smiled at her in return and then gathered their cups and saucers and placed them on the tea tray with the plate of cookies.

As she stood, tray in her hands, Betty looked up at her as she eased herself to her feet. "You're right, of course. It might very well be someone we know. There are many people in our community who need a helping hand. Those who've lost their jobs, have medical bills to pay, groceries to buy, and then there are kids who want what they or their parents can't afford—the latest electronic gadget or super-duper cell phone." She sighed. "Assuming the word did get out, really, it could have been anyone."

"Bob Hiller," Mary said softly, blinking. "You don't suppose, because of his granddaughter, he might do something like this?"

Betty's eyes grew wide. "Oh dear," she said. "He was quite distraught tonight."

"If he did such a thing, he stands to lose so much—his job, his standing in the community, his personal integrity." Mary remembered the lines on his face, the sorrow in his eyes. "On the other hand, maybe he would think it the morally correct thing to do—to take care of a child with great need. A child of his own flesh and blood. A child he already tried to make a big sacrifice for by donating a kidney." Mary fell silent for a moment and then added softly, "If this could be true, why didn't he just ask?"

"That's a good point." Betty started for the kitchen, but when she reached the doorway, she turned and set down the tray. "We both have known Bob for a long time. There's not a dishonest bone in his body."

"The kind of love he has for his granddaughter, though . . . That kind of desperation—" Mary began.

"Might change a person," Betty finished, her expression sad. "I know."

A short time later, Mary slipped into bed and leaned back against her pillows, still lost in thought. Outside, the gentle rain fell on the roof with a comforting rhythm. She opened her Bible and turned to the twentieth Psalm (NKJV) to quiet her spirit. When she reached verse four, she stopped reading to dwell on the words: "May he grant you according to your heart's desire, and fulfill all your purpose."

"Lord," she whispered, "You know my heart's desire, and You know that I want to fulfill Your purpose in my life. The unknown looms before me, yet I know You see all things, that nothing surprises You. Help me figure out the mystery of the book's disappearance.

"More than anything, Father, I pray for little Isabella and her parents—and her grandfather Bob. I know his heart aches for his little Isabella. The family's need is so great, and the sale of this book would make a huge difference in their lives."

She put away her Bible and turned out her bedside light. For a moment, she laid there, listening to the rain. The search for the book that turned up nothing, the puzzling mystery—and the delight she usually took in solving one—meant so little right now. Little Isabella and her parents, Gabriel and Amanda, and even her grandfather Bob Hiller were what mattered most.

"May Your loving presence be with us all this night, Lord, especially with Isabella," she whispered.

The next morning, Mary swung her legs over the side of the bed, reached for her robe and slippers, and moved to the window. After pulling back the curtain, she peered out. The storm had passed through, leaving the predawn sky a rosy pearl gray. Rays of light from the coming sunrise touched the barren trees, reflecting off the remaining droplets of rain. "Joy indeed comes in the morning," Mary whispered. "Thank You, Lord. I think I'm ready to face whatever this day may bring."

Her thoughts turned to the mystery of the book's disappearance, and more important, to Isabella and her needs. She stood silently for a moment, praying for the little girl and her family before going downstairs to call Orris.

Betty came into the kitchen just as Mary ended the call to Orris Rathburn.

At Betty's questioning look, Mary said, "He's disappointed but didn't mention a word of blame. I worried he might think

I wasn't careful enough with the book. He asked if there was anything he could do on his end." She poured a cup of coffee for Betty and another for herself. They settled into their usual places at the kitchen table.

"He's well connected in Weston and here," Betty said. "Known to be a levelheaded businessman. A good person to deal with." Betty had recommended Orris to Mary based on the advice of a few women in her book club.

Mary felt a smile start to take over her face. "Aha, Bets. Maybe that's a dot that needs to be connected. Perhaps the word about the sale got out through his agency and spread from there."

Betty seemed to consider this as she took a sip of coffee. "If so, I doubt that it was done on purpose. The company is reputable. The women in my book club who have used Orris Rathburn have been quite pleased with his services." She smiled. "And you know how picky they are."

Betty's book-club friends and probably many others. Mary turned the thought over in her mind a few times, and she made a mental note to investigate who else in Ivy Bay might have a connection. The important thing was Orris Rathburn and his company had dealings with others in Ivy Bay. She nibbled on her bottom lip for a moment as she considered it. At the very least, that knowledge opened the field of suspects considerably.

Betty gave her a quizzical look. "Something tells me the wheels are beginning to spin."

Mary laughed lightly. "You know me well."

"That I do."

"You've given me something to mull over," Mary said, standing to retrieve the coffee carafe. "Do you want some more?"

Betty shook her head. "I need to be on my way." A hint of a pleased smile curved her lips. "I have a job to do this morning."

Mary had noticed her sister was dressed quite smartly for a weekday morning. "Where are you headed?"

"I didn't have a chance to tell you with all the goings-on yesterday, but Alexa Rose, owner of our new bed-and-breakfast, asked me to help her decorate the cottage."

"The Chickadee?"

"That's the one." Betty's smile widened. "Someone she ran into at the Tea Shoppe told her about how much she liked the way I decorate. She actually asked what I would charge." Betty laughed lightly. "I didn't quite know what to say to that and finally we agreed on expenses only."

Mary laughed with her sister. Betty certainly didn't need the money, but the fact that someone thought her a professional and wanted to hire her must have felt good. She was proud of Betty. "You do have a knack for decorating. I love that you'll have a chance to show it off."

Betty chuckled. "She did lay down one rule. She really wants books available in her guest rooms and worked into the decor—she said it was a priority—but she gave the caveat that they must be of the 'highest literary quality.' And the covers must match the colors in the room."

Mary raised a brow. "Really? Did she define 'literary'?"

"Only by what she doesn't like..."

"Such as?"

"She especially dislikes mysteries of any kind."

Mary sat forward, a smile playing at the corners of her lips. "You're kidding. Does she know your sister owns and operates a mystery bookshop?"

Betty's eyes twinkled. "She didn't until I told her." She headed toward the door, then turned, her expression serious. "Did Chief McArthur call?"

"No, not yet. But he said he didn't know how soon he could get someone over." Her countenance fell as her focus turned back to the need to find the book. And find it fast.

Mary thought about the new Chickadee Inn on her way to the bookshop. Mary looked forward to meeting the owner Alexa Rose and playfully schemed to introduce the woman to some of the finest mysteries ever written. She smiled as she headed to the shop, thinking of titles and authors that might appeal to someone new to the genre.

And she wondered if Alexa knew that some of the most celebrated literary classics written in the last century had strong elements of mystery in them. Books such as Daphne du Maurier's *Rebecca* or *My Cousin Rachel*. Who could not keep turning pages after reading, "When the leaves rustle, they sound very much like the stealthy movement of a woman in evening dress, and when they shiver suddenly, and fall, and scatter away along the ground, they might be the patter, patter of a woman's hurrying footsteps, and the mark in the gravel the imprint of a high-heeled satin shoe"?

She continued to the bookshop, her mind returning to the mystery of the missing book. She drove a few blocks on Main Street when a black BMW came roaring out of nowhere. For a brief moment, she thought the driver might ram the rear of her vehicle. She slammed on her brakes and swerved to the side of the road.

The black BMW roared past, and she gasped.

Nigel Finnian!

Mary only caught a glimpse of Nigel from the shoulders up as he whizzed by, but he looked slumped and forlorn, even angry, judging by the jut of his chin. Yes, definitely angry. The shadow of dark stubble covered his jaw, his shoulders were slumped, and his mouth was set rigid in a line.

Immediately, the events of the night before filled Mary's mind. Could he have been the one who took the book? Was it in his possession now? If so, where was he taking it?

Mary watched the gleaming black car speed around the corner. If she moved fast, she could perhaps find out. She pulled away from the curb and followed at a distance.

Where was he heading? It didn't take long to find out. Within a minute or two, he pulled into the Chickadee Inn. Mary slowed her car to a crawl as she passed, and held her breath, hoping he wouldn't turn toward her. Thankfully, he didn't.

Nigel exited his car and headed for the bed-and-breakfast door. Mary pulled over and parked behind a thick stand of sea grass, and then she got out and crept closer to the cottage. The voices of Nigel and Alexa carried toward her....

"No," Alexa said. "No one fitting that description has checked in here."

"Are you sure?"

"I'm certain." She sounded irritated.

"She was expected late yesterday evening."

"Both bridges were out—downed trees. It caused delays for other guests too. Crews worked on it during the night, so I think it's passable now."

"You'll call when she arrives?"

"I've already given you more information than I should have. I honor my guests' privacy."

"This is important. It's regarding the death of..."

Their voices faded as the woman invited Nigel to step inside. The door closed, and for Mary, that was the end of the conversation.

The death of whom?

———

It was a few minutes before nine when Mary let herself in the bookshop and flipped on the lights. She set down Gus's carrier, opened the door, and watched him scamper off. She thought better of leaving her purse in its usual place for now—although she was sure she'd eventually settle back into the routine, knowing there was no use for perpetual paranoia—and headed to the rear of the shop to leave it in a cupboard in the back room. She pulled out her cell phone and dropped it into the front pocket of her khakis.

After turning on the fire, she straightened shelves and books, and then returned to the back room for the feather duster.

She was prioritizing the morning's tasks—moving anything having to do with the mystery to the top of the list—when her cell phone rang. She pulled it from her pocket and answered it.

"Mary, it's Rebecca."

It was unusual for her employee to call just before she was expected in. "Is everything okay?"

"Oh yes." She could hear the smile in Rebecca's voice. "I just wondered if it's okay to bring Aunt Millicent with me today. I'm worried she'll be lonely all cooped up in the house by herself, with Ashley at school and Russell at work."

"Yes, of course. I'd love to have her."

"She says she'll be no trouble. She loves to crochet and has several projects she's working on right now."

"Tell her I'm looking forward to seeing her."

Mary went back to her dusting, her spirits lifting as she dusted Betty's display in the front window. Betty had used her own teapot collection from around the world that included all sizes, shapes, designs, and colors. *Winter Warmth* was spelled out in a warm oak block lettering in the center, atop a length of pure white quilt batting that gave the appearance of snow. Betty had placed the teapots near plates of homemade dough "cookies," inedible, but looking good enough to eat, and baskets of various kinds of wintry teas; and she'd artistically stacked some cozy mysteries with a teatime theme, in twos or threes, near a few of the teapots. Standing upright behind the display were two delightful Fancy Nancy children's picture books about how to put on a tea party. Twinkling white lights framed the edges of the window, the perfect finishing touch.

Since Betty had put up the new window display right after she removed the antique nativity display, they'd laughed at how many people had wanted to buy one of the teapots, thinking they were for sale. She'd also sold several of the teatime mysteries. Mary was pleased that Betty's unique window displays had captured the attention of nearly everyone who passed by and were often the warm and inviting catalyst that brought them into the shop.

As she lifted the pots one by one to dust, she waved to friends from the nearby shops and other walkers who paused to look at the display. She was glad to see people were out and about after the fierce storm and was even happier that they continued to enjoy Betty's unique artistry.

Jayne Tucker waved at Mary as she stopped to look. As owners of Gems and Antiques, Jayne and her husband Rich were getting ready for their annual trip to Europe to search for gems and antiques to bring back to sell.

Jayne moved on, and Susan Crosby, owner of Sweet Susan's Bakery next door, stepped out of her front door, looked over at Mary, smiled, and toodled her fingers.

Mary unlocked the door, and Susan, holding a covered tray with one hand, popped her head in. The fragrance of apple and cinnamon from the baked goods she carried filled the bookshop.

"Just wanted to say a quick good morning," Susan said. "That was quite a storm last night. Did you have any damage?"

"No, just a power outage."

"Same with us. I came in early to make sure the ovens are working." She grinned. "And thank goodness, they are."

Susan stepped away from the shop and headed to her car. She sometimes made impromptu deliveries of her signature cupcakes to shut-ins. Mary loved that about her.

Mary's phone rang again, and she pulled it from her pocket once more. The caller ID made her smile. It was her daughter Elizabeth. "Hi, Lizzie."

"How did the book chat go last night? I saw on the news that you got hit hard by the winds. Are you and Aunt Betty okay?"

"We're fine," Mary said, wondering if she should tell her daughter about the missing book. She didn't want her to worry, but her daughter might hear the concern in her voice and wonder what was wrong. She continued dusting, still holding the phone to her ear, trying to decide.

"Mom...?"

"I'm here, honey."

"Something is wrong. I can tell."

Mary laughed lightly. "I was just debating whether to tell you."

"What is it?"

Mary told her about the book, starting with the phone call from Orris Rathburn and ending with the visit from Chief McArthur. And the fact that when he arrived, the book was missing.

Lizzie let out a long sigh. "Mom, you could have been injured. What if the robber had been there when you arrived last night?"

Mary laughed. "Now, honey, that's why I was debating with myself about telling you. Please don't worry. I'm in no danger. I just want to find the book."

Lizzie sighed again. "Promise me you won't take any chances...."

"Of course I won't."

"I need to get to school. I'm volunteering in Luke's classroom this morning."

"You run along. I'll let you know when I get to the bottom of this."

"Promise?"

"Promise."

It was nearly ten when she moved to the bookshelves, feather duster still in hand, starting with the children's nook.

Just then, the bell above the front door jingled. Gus looked up from his snooze on the hearth, eyes wide, ears forward.

Mary turned toward the door from her awkward position in the children's tub—an antique bathtub that Betty had carpeted to create a cozy reading space for the kiddos—and Rebecca was there, giggling. "You should have let me do that," she said.

"Nah, a little elbow grease does a body good," Mary said as she pulled herself out of her tub. She smiled at Millicent, who'd entered just after Rebecca. "Hello again, Millicent. Good to see you this morning."

"I promise I won't be any trouble," Millicent said as she followed her grandniece farther into the store, working her cane with each step. She moved closer to Mary, who was now dusting the rocking chair in the nook. "Oh, I just adore that rocking chair. I noticed it last night." Her white curls bobbed as she spoke. "They're so good for the back, you know. Maybe I'll just sit myself right there and crochet, if that's all right with you."

"Better yet, how about if we move the rocking chair to the fireplace—just for you while you're here?" Mary said.

Millicent smiled. Instead of eightysomething, she looked more like sixty. Mary could see that she must have been a stunning beauty in her day. She was still striking.

"This was my grandmother's rocking chair," Mary said, and she and Rebecca placed it in front of the fireplace. "I'm happy that you can enjoy it."

Aunt Millicent settled into the rocker, her needlework tote at her side. Gus walked over, turned around three times, finally settled near the rocker and closed his eyes with a low, contented purr.

"Your shop is so welcoming," Millicent said to Mary, looking around with obvious appreciation. "And the teapot collection in the window is exquisite. I noticed it last night when I first arrived. It's set off just right with those twinkling lights. I especially love the Mary Engelbreit teapot." She reached out as if to touch it and then drew back her hand. "Are the teapots for sale?"

"The collection belongs to my sister Betty. We're using them just as window decoration. If you'd like to have a closer look, though, I can show them to you."

Millicent's expression grew wistful. "My husband started a collection for me long before he passed. I've always treasured it."

Millicent smiled, but Mary's heart went out to her. Mary knew the raw emotion of losing someone you'd loved for decades, with whom you'd raised children together, dreamed dreams together, nursed each other through illness, celebrated grandchildren, cried together in difficult times, rejoiced together in the good times. Then all at once, the one you'd loved for what seemed like forever was gone. She touched Millicent's hand, and the older woman grasped Mary's hand in return and gave it a light squeeze.

Rebecca stood nearby and mouthed a thank-you. It struck Mary how good it was of Rebecca to invite her elderly aunt into her home to try to heal and work through her devastating loss. The act spoke volumes about Rebecca's character, although Mary already knew how good a heart Rebecca had.

She smiled at the young woman, so glad—once again—that Rebecca had come to her for a job so soon after the shop opened. Rebecca's skills at running the shop were impressive, and her knowledge of books never ceased to amaze Mary. Her precocious daughter Ashley was a bookworm as well, and a pleasure to have around when she wasn't in school.

"We need to work on inventory today," Mary said to Rebecca as they walked to the storeroom. "At least between customers."

Rebecca laughed. "And after last night's storm, I'm guessing we'll have a run on books. People stocking up for the next nor'easter."

"I'd love to help out if needed," Millicent called to them, her hearing obviously not at all challenged by her advanced age.

Mary exchanged grins with Rebecca.

"Just let me know if there's anything I can do. Though I did bring plenty of busywork along."

"She crochets beautiful baby prayer blankets and darling hats for women undergoing chemo. She made a thousand hats in one year, she told me. She's got a heart of pure gold." She grinned. "Make that platinum—it's better than gold."

Mary went over for a closer look at what appeared to be a baby blanket as Millicent proudly pulled it from her bag, then reached in for her crochet hook and some scissors. Mary caught a glimpse of several skeins of yarn in the bag, but none were the color of the piece of yarn she'd discovered on the floor by the cash register the day before.

Millicent began to work and became quickly engrossed in her project, and Mary went back to the front to chat with Rebecca.

Mary lowered her voice and told her employee what had happened after she returned from dropping off Heidi. "I couldn't have been gone more than fifteen or twenty minutes. And everything was locked when I left."

Rebecca's dismay showed in her expression. "Oh no," she whispered. She put her hand to her cheek and closed her eyes as if giving her heart time to process the information.

"You think it's the same person who tried to take it earlier yesterday?"

"I honestly don't know, but it seems likely."

"Could it have been taken when the lights went out?" Rebecca said, her forehead furrowed in worry. "There were a number of people crowded around the front door and window, also the counter during that time."

"I've thought about that too," Mary said. "I've gone over the list of people who were there—some we knew, others we didn't. I haven't wanted to consider that any of our book chat guests might do such a thing, but I've had to."

"What did the chief say?"

"He's sending someone over to look around, see if there's anything we missed. There were a couple of things left that may or may not be clues," Mary said. "I'm not sure what they mean."

"What are they?"

"A man's comb. It looked old. Maybe an antique. It had a word, perhaps initials partially worn off, on the silver backing."

"There's only one man I can think of who was here last night who might have something like that."

Mary couldn't help smiling. "It wasn't the sort of thing Bob or Henry would carry, that's for sure. I've seen Henry take a comb out to run through his hair, and it was as plain a comb as can be, but I've never seen Bob or Clayton do it."

"They both usually wear hats."

"True." Mary narrowed her eyes in thought. "Which leaves one man it might belong to," Rebecca said.

Mary nodded. "Nigel Finnian." Mary pictured the angle someone would have to sit for a comb to fall out of a pants pocket. Sit wasn't the right word. He would have to squat to search for the key and open the cupboard. She remembered that he'd squatted to pick up Gus. Was that reason enough to let him off the hook?

"What else did you find?" Rebecca looked worried.

"A piece of yarn, though it was probably from one of Gus's toys." She gave Rebecca a wry smile. "Several of his catnip mice have missing tails, and they're just the same neutral tone as the yarn I found. And then there was something else. A scrap of paper that appeared to have been torn from a business planner page or personal calendar. A portion of the lettering showed it was from January. But no date."

She kept her voice low, glanced over at Millicent in the back of the store who was counting stitches and appeared completely engrossed, and then glanced back to Rebecca. As much as she liked Millicent, she didn't know whether the woman had a penchant for gossip, and Mary wanted to keep this theft as quiet as possible. "I did think to take a picture of the comb with my phone, though."

Rebecca's eyes brightened. "Can I have a look?"

"Sure. Maybe you'll recognize it."

Mary glanced at Millicent who was still counting a row of double crochet stitches. Perhaps recounting. Mary knew from experience how easy it was to get mixed up with such a thing. She'd been knitting the same scarf for years.

Rebecca frowned as she examined the photos of the comb. She shook her head slowly and handed them back to Mary.

"I know it's been only hours since the book was taken, but I keep thinking there's more to it than what meets the eye," Mary said, and then she laughed. "Of course, there always is, isn't there?"

Rebecca leaned against the counter, her expression still troubled. "Could someone have slipped in the back door during the power outage?"

"I suppose so," Mary said, "although with so many people looking for flashlights, lanterns, old lamps, and such in the back room and downstairs, I think one of you would have heard or seen someone coming in." A hesitant knock sounded at the front door, interrupting Mary's thoughts. She glanced at her watch. She'd been so engrossed in the mystery she'd forgotten to turn the Open sign around. She turned to see Hazel Pritchard standing at the door. She gave the woman a rueful wave.

Rebecca laughed lightly, understanding. "I'll get the door."

Mary loved that Rebecca didn't hang back waiting to be told what to do.

As Rebecca headed over to greet Hazel, a small woman with gray hair and a cane, Mary picked up the feather duster, planning to finish the shelves she'd started earlier.

She looked up as Chief McArthur arrived in his cruiser. A detective pulled up behind him and got out of his vehicle.

SEVEN

I'm sorry, Mary," the chief said. They stood just outside her shop in the late morning sunshine. The detective had just pulled away. "I'd hoped that maybe I'd overlooked something last night. But there's really no more light to shed on this thing. That doesn't mean we'll stop sending out feelers. Whoever took a book of this value may be trying to get rid of it quickly. Get the money and run, so to speak."

Mary's heart fell.

"Again, we need to consider that it might have been an inside job. Someone who had a key. No locks were jimmied, indoors or out. And as I mentioned, it would have been easy enough for someone to take your keys."

Inside job. Just hearing the words spoken reminded her that one of the Winter Warmth Book Chat guests might have taken it. Especially Nigel Finnian. The others were people she knew personally, or were known by people she trusted. Such as Rebecca's Aunt Millicent.

"What about the office of Orris Rathburn, the dealer I was going to sell the book to?" she said. "I've wondered if somehow the word got out through his colleagues."

"Good thinking. He's from where...again?"

"Weston, a suburb of Boston."

The chief wrote it in his notebook.

"I don't mean to accuse Mr. Rathburn himself. He'd already made the agreement with a buyer. He'd have nothing to gain—actually, he'd have a lot to lose."

"But someone in his office could have spread the word," the chief said.

"That's what I was thinking."

Chief McArthur leaned one elbow on the countertop. "We've got to follow every lead. And consider everyone who might be a suspect." His demeanor sobered. "This is grand theft we're talking about, you know." He scanned the street as a few cars passed by. "I'll get an investigation going on the Weston end of things."

"Thank you, Chief."

"Is there anything else?"

She shook her head. She didn't feel she had enough evidence to mention any of her suspects to the chief. *Enough* evidence? She really didn't have any. She was still connecting dots.

The chief gave her a serious look. "Call me if you hear anything."

"I will."

He got into his vehicle, backed out of the parking space, and drove off.

The chief had just pulled away when Heidi and Cade roared around the corner on his motorcycle. Heidi waved gaily as Cade drew to a stop.

Mary whispered a quick prayer for the young mother-to-be's safety as she opened the door and let Heidi enter the bookshop.

"Is it okay to stop by right now? I'd really love to take you up on your offer and get some help with my reading. If you have time, I mean," she said timidly.

She looked expectantly at Mary, who nodded, pleased with the girl's initiative. "Of course. We're happy to have you stop by." At that, Heidi turned to wave to her husband through the window. He blew her a kiss and grinned as he roared away, the sound of the engine reverberating through the street.

Mary knew she needed to tell Heidi about the missing book. If Heidi had stolen it, she may be inclined to return the book if she knew the purpose Mary'd had for the book's proceeds.

Heidi smiled at Mary once more, then started to head back toward the fireplace where Millicent was seated, but Mary quickly intercepted her.

"How was your evening last night, after the book chat?" Mary started, hoping Heidi would return the question.

"Oh, it was nice," Heidi said, pivoting slightly back toward Mary. "I was buzzing after our chat, so Cade and I played cribbage, then headed to bed. Not too exciting, but good," Heidi said with a chuckle. "How about your evening?"

Mary allowed her disappointment about the book to show on her face. "I wish I could say it was a good evening, but sadly, something unfortunate happened. I was storing a valuable book here that I had just accepted a bid on, but it was stolen." Heidi's face registered instant shock, which to Mary meant Heidi was either innocent or she had forced herself to fake it. "I wouldn't really care, except that the money from the sale was meant to help pay the bills for Isabella Hiller's kidney transplant."

"Oh no!" Heidi said, her face panged with guilt. Whether the guilt was over her actions or over heartache for Isabella, Mary couldn't discern. "How awful!"

"It is." Although Mary wanted Heidi to know about the book, she wasn't sure she necessarily wanted the news to travel around town. "If you could keep that information in your confidence, though," Mary said to Heidi, whose chin rose a bit. Heidi looked both surprised and proud to have had Mary confide in her.

"Of course," Heidi said seriously. "Please let me know if you need anything."

"Thank you," Mary said, studying the girl but feeling unable to read her.

Millicent was crocheting by the fireplace and called for Heidi to sit by her. Heidi gave Mary a soft smile, then headed toward the back of the store.

Mary walked with her to prepare the girl a cup of hot chocolate.

Heidi sat in one of the easy chairs near the fireplace.

"It's so nice to see you again, Heidi," Millicent said.

"You too," Heidi said. "I actually came to learn to read better. Mary has generously opened her shop to me." Her cheeks were pink with either embarrassment or the delight of being in the bookshop again. Because Heidi's gaze kept darting to the children's nook, Mary suspected it was the latter.

Millicent noticed too. "I see. Well, someday, you'll have the thrill of reading to your baby. Children's books are some of my favorites." She laughed. "Imagine, such a thing at my age. I adore the C. S. Lewis Narnia series." She leaned forward conspiratorially. "I wouldn't mind it if you'd pick up a copy of *The Lion, the Witch, and the Wardrobe* and read it to me…. It would be good practice for you for later. And I'd love it."

"Really?" Heidi blinked, and Mary was thrilled. Regardless of Heidi's potential guilt, this seemed like a perfect partnership. It gave Millicent something to do and Heidi a way to learn. Mary handed the cup to Heidi, and the young woman thanked her.

"I would love it." Millicent sat back. She exchanged smiles with Mary and gave her a slight nod as she headed to the front of the shop.

The day passed pleasantly as Heidi read in the background while Millicent listened patiently, helping Heidi with pronunciation from time to time and commenting on the story line. Mary was charmed by Millicent and thought it would be nice to invite Millicent and Rebecca over for dinner, but she'd check with Betty first.

Rebecca came out from the back room where she was unpacking an order of books and grinned at her aunt.

"Do you mind if I go to lunch? I'd like to take Aunt Millicent with me to the shanty I write in, show her what I've been up to." Rebecca often took her lunch in a fisherman's shanty, which she'd set up as a writing retreat. "She said she would enjoy seeing it."

"Not at all," Mary said. She checked her watch. "Do you want to go now?"

"If it's all right."

Millicent broke in, obviously having overheard, which made Mary wonder how much of the day's other conversations she'd listened in on.

"You go on, dear," she said to Rebecca. "I'm quite comfy staying here. Just leave me that sandwich you packed this morning, and I'll be happy as a clam." She smiled at Heidi. "It's big enough for two, if you'd like to share."

"Well, thank you...," Heidi said hesitantly. "But I can only stay a few more minutes. I need to get home to fix lunch for Cade."

Mary expected Millicent to change her mind since she'd no longer have Heidi to keep her company. But she said she'd be content to stay right where she was, rocking and crocheting by the fire. "Why don't you go ahead too?" she said to Mary, then shrugged and laughed at the notion. "As if I could run this place while you're gone...." Her voice drifted off as she looked around, her eyes suddenly looking sad. Mary wondered if she was thinking of other times and other places when she was younger and such a thing would have been possible. "Just a thought," Millicent said, going back to her crocheting. "I could help out if you needed me to," she added softly, almost as if to herself.

"We sometimes get people coming in on their lunch breaks," Mary said gently. "It can get pretty hectic. But there's quite a bit of training involved. It would be almost impossible to do without it."

"I understand," Millicent said, looking down as she made another stitch.

As it turned out, the shop was even busier than Mary predicted, plus between two customers, her son Jack called to make sure Mary was okay. It was obvious that Lizzie had called him after she'd talked to Mary earlier. He was between patients and obviously busy—Mary could hear the background noise of fussing toddlers and crying babies in his waiting room—but Jack sounded relieved when he heard her voice.

Rebecca didn't take as long a lunch break as Mary expected, seeming concerned about getting back to her aunt. When she came back, she drew Mary aside in the back room. "I'm worried about Aunt Millicent," she said. "She seems to tear up at the slightest thing. And she's eating very little." Her worried gaze met Mary's. "Did she eat her sandwich?"

"A few bites, and then I fixed her some tea. But don't worry. What she's going through is natural. It just takes time to get through the grieving process, believe me." Mary smiled at her employee. "And please, don't worry that she'll bother me when she's here. She's pleasant to the customers, and I think what she's doing for Heidi is just what she needs."

"What they *both* need," Rebecca said.

Mary left the shop soon after. All morning, the theft of the treasured book had been lurking just beneath the surface of her emotions.

She needed some time to gather her thoughts and to pray. Before heading home for lunch, she drove out toward the harbor for a cruise along the coast. She pulled over to a wide spot overlooking the dunes, got out of the car, glad for her coat and scarf, and gazed out at the sparkling water. The wind was brisk, creating a chop of white wavelets sparkling in the sunlight. Tree branches, downed by the winds the night before, were scattered across the sand, but her eyes lifted from the tumbled debris of the storm's aftermath to the calm horizon. In the sand, patches of ice created patches of dull sheen that reflected the sky.

Leaning against the car, she drew in a deep breath. Though the air was bitter cold, the beauty of the place settled her soul, brought peace and calm. At the heart of the mystery was a place of pain, specifically the sadness she felt for little Isabella—and her growing sense of helplessness to find the book that would help the child.

"Lord, nothing is lost from You," she whispered into the wind. "Not a child. Not a book. Nothing." She pondered the thought, feeling a great weight lift from her shoulders. "You are with me as I try to figure out this troubling puzzle. You are with precious little Isabella, her mom and dad. You know their needs better than they do, than any of us do. We know from Your Word that there is never a moment that You remove Your attention from us."

She looked out at the water again. "Help me find the book, Father. Help me think clearly."

She got back in the car, pulled out her cell phone, and dialed Bob Hiller. When he answered, she asked if he remembered the street address that Nigel Finnian had inquired about the night before.

"Oh yes," he said, "I remember it well." He laughed lightly. "Addresses are my specialty." She laughed with him. Of course, as a postman, they certainly ought to be.

"The only trouble is," he said, "the old fishermen's cottages out there are so weathered the numbers often can't be seen, especially from the road. And because some are rentals, folks who live in them have to come into town to the post office for their mail."

"Thank you, Bob. That helps."

There was a pause. Then Bob let out an audible breath. "There's a rumor going around that I wanted to ask you about."

Mary felt her heart almost jolt to a stop.

"About a book that you found."

For a stunned moment, she didn't speak.

"The Agatha Christie book that you bought at a flea market."

She gasped with surprise. "Where did you hear about that?"

"From a few folks. I've known for over a week. I think nearly everyone at the book chat last night had heard about it." He chuckled. "Though no one knows where you're keeping it. But I could see folks craning, trying to get a look at it, but no one wanted to come right out and ask. Then the lights went out, and well, the rest is history, as they say."

"How did you find out?" Her mind was racing.

He laughed again. "Word is that the appraiser was a bit of a blab. Apparently, he was new in the business and bragged to a waitress he was trying to impress in a diner outside of town. Needless to say, he was overheard. At least that's one story that's circulating. There may be others."

Mary was stunned. She sat back, trying to take it in. Nearly everyone there knew about it? It made Chief McArthur's words "inside job" even more relevant. "Where did you hear it?"

"Oh, it was going around the post office, among workers in back and the folks out front. Everyone has been speculating on the value. Someone even said a million dollars, but I thought that was ridiculous. And someone said it contained a map with the exact destination of where Miss Christie went when she disappeared all those years ago."

"Oh dear," Mary said with a sigh. "None of that is true. And its real value is much, much lower than people are speculating."

"Like I said, the appraiser was trying to impress the waitress, or so I heard. Who knows, he could have inflated the value." Bob fell quiet. "Made for a good story, though." His voice took on a somber tone, laced with disappointment, seemingly deep disappointment, when he continued. "I think all of us wanted it to be worth a million."

She wondered if the disappointment she'd heard had been her imagination, or if she really did hear something more than a friend's commiseration. But there was more to it than just her worries about Bob and his tone; the exaggeration of a million-dollar price tag was as silly as it was a possible motive for someone to have committed the crime.

Mary dropped her forehead into her hand, wondering whether she should tell Bob about the theft. So far, he assumed she still had the book in her possession. Or did he? She couldn't eliminate him as a suspect, and until she could, she needed to keep mum.

"I've been praying for Isabella every day," she said, changing the subject. "Tell her I'll be by another day soon for a visit." She had been by the hospital to visit Isabella and her family a few times, taking books from the shop. The child was as voracious a reader as Ashley was. She especially liked Junie B. Jones.

"She'll love that," Bob said. "Thanks again for the books. She talks incessantly about them." He paused, and for a moment, Mary worried one of their phones had disconnected. When he continued, his voice was gruff. "I can't imagine what it's like for an active little girl to have to go through this staying-in-bed business. It's heartbreaking for me to see. But I thank you for what you and other friends are doing to keep her mind busy. She loves to read, and the books you brought really made her face light up."

"I'm happy to do what I can," Mary said. "We all are."

"I know," Bob said. "I know."

Mary heard the anxiety in his voice, and she whispered another prayer for Bob and for the entire family.

As they said their good-byes, she again wondered if Bob, out of love for his grandchild, might have crossed the line between right and wrong. She hoped not, but neither could she rule out the possibility.

She arrived home a few minutes later. Betty's car was parked in the driveway, so she swung around and parked in the street.

As she stepped out of the car, she couldn't help but admire, not for the first time, the stately homes that made up Betty's neighborhood. They were separated by enough space to provide privacy and comfort, but close enough to encourage a lovely sense of community, something that Mary cherished. Nearly everyone maintained their properties beautifully, even in the cold of winter, and the crispness of the blanketed landscaping made the scene look as if it was straight from a Christmas painting.

Already, cleanup from the windstorm was well under way, branches picked up and disposed of, walkways swept, and yards raked. Come spring, the yards would be filled with a riot of color as the large lush trees and lush foliage burst into bloom.

Tom Waterford, the owner of the *Ivy Bay Bugle*, lived across the street and was outside. His wife Marjorie drove down the street and waved at Mary before turning into her driveway. Mary smiled and waved back, glad for a neighborhood—and neighbors—who cared about one another.

Betty was putting together tea sandwiches for lunch, and soup was simmering on the stove when Mary came inside. "I hope cream cheese and chopped olives work for you," her sister said as Mary entered the kitchen.

"Nothing sounds better," Mary said. Betty winced as she reached for the soup bowls, and Mary hurriedly put her purse down so she could help. "How did your morning go?" Mary said as she carried the bowls to the table.

Betty rolled her eyes. "Oh my. Alexa is going to be a challenge. Pretty as a Dresden doll but stubborn as Paul Bunyan's blue ox." Her eyes twinkled. "But a good challenge."

Mary laughed as she sat and reached for her napkin. Betty sat across from her and bowed her head. "It's your turn," she said.

After Mary said grace, she told her sister about following Nigel to the bed-and-breakfast, talking to Chief McArthur, and then finding out from Bob Hiller that nearly everyone in town knew about the book. She stopped to take a breath, and Betty chuckled.

"I saw Nigel at the bed-and-breakfast too. He and Alexa spoke for a few minutes at the reception desk, but I couldn't hear them. He left soon after." She frowned as she unfolded her napkin. "There was something furtive about the way they dropped their voices. It made me wonder why."

Mary reached for her napkin and dabbed at the corners of her mouth. "I spotted him just before you did, then, while they were still outside. It sounded like he was trying to force Alexa to give him information about a guest—someone who was supposed to arrive last night but couldn't because of a closed road.

"He wasn't asking forcefully but certainly with a bit of a, well, threatening tone. And you should see the way he looks today. None of that debonair, man-about-town look we saw last night. He looked, well, unkempt."

"Maybe because he couldn't find his comb." Betty quirked an eyebrow.

"I hope I'm not sounding melodramatic," Mary said, a smile playing at the corners of her lips.

Betty laughed and patted her sister's hand. "Not a bit melodramatic. You know very well how you've brightened things up for me since you moved here. Sometimes your life reads like a mystery itself." She reached for another sandwich.

Mary took a bite of her sandwich, chewed thoughtfully for a moment, and then said, "Millicent looked a little lonely and sad this morning. Rebecca is worried about her. She perked up when she spent time helping Heidi with her reading. And when she spotted your teapot collection, she almost glowed. She said it was a reminder of one that she has—her husband apparently bought several for her through the years."

"Widowhood is hard," Betty said softly. "We both know that firsthand."

"I thought it would be nice to invite Millicent to dinner tonight," Mary said. "I think it might help her to be with us. Maybe we can encourage her somehow." Mary smiled softly. "Perhaps just remind her that life goes on." She paused. "With Rebecca and Ashley, of course, and Russell if he'd like to join us."

Betty's eyes twinkled. "I have the feeling a girls' night out wouldn't be quite his cup of tea."

Mary chuckled. Rebecca's husband Russell was a gruff but good-hearted fisherman, the kind of man who seemed more comfortable on a boat or at his own kitchen table than just about anywhere. "I'll ask, and it'll be up to him."

"Sounds good. It will be fun."

"We've got a chicken casserole in the freezer. I'll come home a little early to put it in the oven."

"Don't forget to take it out to thaw," Betty said, and she stood to take her dishes to the sink. She winked at Mary just before she headed through the kitchen door.

Mary rolled her eyes. Betty never forgot she was the older sister, even if it was only by two years.

As Mary rummaged through the freezer shelves for the casserole, her thoughts turned to Isabella. She made a mental note to stop by the hospital with the new stack of Junie B. Jones books she'd gathered and tucked into a colorful Disney princess tote and left in her car.

It also struck her that Isabella was the same age as Ashley, in the same grade at school.

As she placed the fresh-from-the-freezer baking dish on the counter, she whispered another prayer for Isabella and her parents.

And for herself. That she would not get discouraged in her search for the stolen book.

EIGHT

The kitchen was filled with a wonderful scent of bubbling Chicken Divan, with layers of bite-sized pieces of cooked chicken breast and steamed broccoli, covered with a sauce of sour cream, shredded cheddar, cream of mushroom soup, melted butter, and then Mary's secret ingredients: a squeeze of lemon and a teaspoon of curry. She had just started making the salad when Betty came in, shaking her head slowly.

Mary put the lettuce into the colander to drain. "Is everything all right?"

Betty almost collapsed into a chair at the table, sighed, and playfully rolled her eyes. "This dear woman is one of a kind."

"Alexa?"

Her sister nodded. "She keeps insisting that every element of the decor be 'highbrow.' She's reminded me numerous times that the books on display need to be literary only, no mysteries. It will be no problem for me to find the kinds of books she wants; I just think it's curious. What does she have against mysteries? Especially considering that almost every novel has some elements of mystery."

"It is a little strange, that's for sure." Mary tore the lettuce into pieces and dropped it into a wooden bowl and then started chopping some green onions.

"Here's an idea," Betty said. "What if we have tea together at the bed-and-breakfast? I think you'd get a kick out of Alexa, actually. And I do tend to wonder if there's something beneath the veneer. Maybe Detective Mary can draw it out of her."

"Well, I don't know about that, but I'd certainly love to have tea. It'll be fun to get to know her better. And just in case," Mary gave Betty a conspiratorial look, "I'll bring along a few of my favorite mysteries for her. You know, if the subject comes up. Handpicked for highest quality, of course."

"Of course," Betty said, a twinkle in her eye. "I'll talk to her soon, and we'll make a date."

"Sounds great. Although I think I may stop by tomorrow, anyway. I am hoping Alexa might be willing to talk about the guest Nigel was asking about, if it doesn't compromise confidentiality. Perhaps I could even make the suggestion of tea to her tomorrow."

"Sounds good to me," Betty said as she put on her apron and grabbed a chef's knife. "Okay, let me at those tomatoes." She took two from the colander and started dicing.

"A new guest checked in this afternoon, by the way," Betty said after a few minutes of silence. "A woman who was quite upset that she couldn't get here 'on time.' I wonder if there's a connection."

Mary stared at her sister for a moment. "The woman that Nigel was asking about?"

"Exactly," Betty said, turning with her hand on her hip. "You think they're connected with the book's disappearance?"

"The words 'on time' strike me as interesting," Mary said, "but the woman could have meant anything by it."

"True."

"I heard Nigel say something odd to Alexa, something about a death, then they went inside." She frowned. "Death of what?"

"Or of who?" Betty studied her. "You look worried."

"I am." She drew in a deep breath and started chopping the cucumber. "What it comes down to is that the person who took the book could be Nigel, but it could also be a friend." She looked up at her sister. "I can't stand the thought that I may not be able to trust the people I care about." She put down the knife and tilted her head. "But you know what? I'm not going to stop trusting my friends. And even more than that—I'm not going to stop trusting them even if I find out they're guilty."

"He giveth more grace," Betty hummed, "as the burdens grow greater..."

When she reached the chorus, Mary warbled along with her quietly, "His love has no limits, His grace has no measure.... He giveth, and giveth, and giveth again." She smiled at Betty. "That song takes me back to our childhood. I've always loved it. Think about it, if God extends His grace so lavishly on us, how can we not do the same to others, no matter what they've done?"

"Even if they've stolen an irreplaceable book?"

"Even then."

"Go get 'em, girl," Betty said, looking proud.

The doorbell rang at six thirty, and Betty headed to the door, and Mary finished placing the napkins on the place mats. The table was set, the casserole was out of the oven, and its fragrance wafted throughout the house. Soon, Rebecca's pleasant laughter, Aunt Millicent's gentle voice, and sweet Ashley's chatter carried from the living room. Mary took off her apron and then hurried in to join them.

Hugs were exchanged, and then she invited them into the kitchen. She asked Ashley to pour the sparkling apple juice, and then they took their places. "Ashley, would you like to ask the blessing for us?" Mary asked.

The child gave Mary an eager smile as she nodded and bowed her head. "Dear God, please bless us all. It would also be great to make this night never end because I love being here so much. And help Isabella to get well soon. Help the doctors know exactly what she needs to heal. Help her mommy and daddy be strong as they wait for her to get better." She paused. "And, oh yes, dear heavenly Father, thank You for the Chicken Divan, though I think it should be called Chicken Divine. Thank You for the tomatoes and cucumbers, though I don't like either very much, and the lettuce and onions and all the nutritious food You give us every day. Amen."

"We made a big card at school for Isabella," Ashley said as her mother dished up a small portion of the casserole onto her plate. "Everybody wrote their names on it. MacKenzie and I glued paper flowers on it, and Jason and Jenny cut out some animals. Then Kathy Lee cut out a round and golden sun, and we glued that on too." She took a drink of the sparkling juice and swallowed a big gulp. "With lots of sunbeams over the house. With all of us working on it, it looked like a mosaic." She sat back and seemed to await a response to the big word.

Mary noticed and raised an eyebrow. "A mosaic, huh?"

Ashley leaned forward. "Yep. It's decorative artwork made by combining small pieces of all kinds of things. It can be made with tiny pieces of colored glass, stone, or paper, which is what we did. Then it's all put together to create a pattern or a picture."

"I'd love to see the card," Mary said. "It sounds like something Isabella will love."

"That's what Mrs. Jacobs said." Ashley sat back and folded her hands.

"I'm so sorry to hear about your friend," Millicent said, her eyes sad. She reached across the table and patted Ashley's hand. "I hope she gets well very soon. Your prayer was very special."

"I'm sorry I didn't think to mention it earlier," Rebecca said. "We were busy at the shop this afternoon, and I just didn't think to tell you. It's been on all our minds since Isabella got sick. The children have missed her a lot."

"How long has she been in the hospital?"

Mary again noticed the tremor in Millicent's hand as she reached for a dinner roll. Mary wondered if she had Parkinson's disease, or if the stress of losing her husband had caused it. Though she seemed to be so used to her beautiful cane that it appeared she'd used it for a long time. That could mean a long-term disease, not a passing stress-related condition. Mary's heart went out to Millicent; she had much to face alone. No wonder she'd come to her grandniece's to soak up some much-needed strength.

"She was admitted a few weeks ago," Mary said and decided it was time to change the subject. "Would anyone like seconds? There's plenty."

"I'll have more lettuce," Ashley said, "but, please, no tomatoes."

Mary dished her up some salad. "How about more chicken *divine*?"

Ashley laughed. "Yes, but, please, I wouldn't care for any fungi." She grinned. "Mushrooms."

Later, after Betty had excused herself to an early bedtime because of increasing arthritis pains, the rest of the group sat in the living room with hot tea and chocolate-chip cookies that Ashley had helped Mary make two weeks earlier. Acting very much in charge, Ashley pulled them out of the freezer, gave them a zap in the microwave to make them fresh-baked warm, and then she placed the plate on the coffee table.

The child cuddled up to Mary on the sofa and sighed. "When do you think Isabella will come home from the hospital?"

"I don't know, honey," Mary said.

"Mrs. Jacobs said that the family needs money to help pay for some new medicine. She put a special jar on her desk, and we all are trying to fill it up with allowances or money we earn. Some of the other classes are selling cookies and cakes and things. They're calling it a bake-off. I thought maybe we could make chocolate-chip cookies again, and I could sell them at the bake-off."

"That's a wonderful idea, honey," Mary said, looking down at her sweet upturned face. "Ask your teacher when you need them, and we'll do it!"

"Good." Ashley reached for Mary's hand and squeezed it tight.

"Is the family having financial difficulties?" Millicent asked. "That's terrible, on top of everything else."

Rebecca chimed in. "All of Ivy Bay is trying to help. They've been putting on rummage sales, taking up special collections at church, that sort of thing, but the need is so much more than what we can give them."

"Would anyone like more tea or cookies?" Mary said, smiling as she stood.

"Oh goodness," Rebecca said, looking at her watch. "We need to be going. It's a school night, and I know a little sleepyhead who needs to get to bed."

Ashley held on to Mary's hand. "I'd rather have a sleepover here."

Mary hugged the child close. "Maybe when we bake more chocolate-chip cookies another time.... How about that?"

Ashley nodded vigorously, and a few minutes later, coats on, the three trooped out the door.

A second later, Ashley turned to look back at Mary. She smiled, opened her arms wide, and ran back to Mary. "I just needed one more hug," she said, squeezing Mary tight around the waist.

It was the best gift Mary could have received as she thought about Isabella and the task ahead: finding the book that would help with her treatment.

Mary knelt and hugged Ashley back, thinking how much Isabella's parents and grandparents prayed for the day they could hug the little one whose health had been restored.

"Hugs are the best," she said. "And a hug from you is one of my very favorites."

NINE

A storm was predicted for later in the week, and when Mary awoke and looked out, clouds in the pink sunrise showed the weather was already changing. She had been awake off and on during the night, puzzling the whereabouts of the book and going through the list in her mind of who might have taken it.

She kept coming back to the timing of the first break-in as well as the second. And bridges. For some reason, she couldn't get the thought of the town's two major bridges out of her mind. Both had been washed out the night of the storm. Something told her they were significant, but why?

She was still pondering the thought when she slipped into her robe and slippers and then padded into the kitchen, poured her coffee, and sat beside Betty at the table.

Betty looked up from her home-decorating magazines, concern in her eyes. "You look tired," she said. "Didn't you sleep well?"

"I did toss and turn a bit last night," Mary admitted. "The missing book is eating at me. I consider suspects, then try to come up with a motive, and greed is not the only thing that comes to me. Compassion is another possible motive."

"Compassion?"

Mary nodded. "It hurts me to say this, but what if it is someone who knows about Isabella's needs—even someone from church—" Again, she thought about the chief's words about it maybe being an inside job.

"We've been praying about Isabella for weeks," Betty said, leaning forward. "Everyone is aware of her physical needs and the financial burden the family is bearing."

"And that their money is about to run out."

Betty swallowed hard. "Yes," she said. "You're right. Compassion could be a motive."

"If you put together the way the news about the book got around town—even though we still don't know for sure how it was originally leaked—with so many people knowing about the book, and the gross exaggeration circulating about its value...And then if you put that together with the needs of the family..." Her voice broke off in a sigh.

"All that's true," Betty said, "but can you discount greed?"

"No, I don't think so. But it's easier to think of greed being a stranger's motive than it is to think of it as one of our friends' motives."

Betty grinned. "This is a lot to take in before I've finished my first coffee." She stood to pour them each another cup.

"The thing is," Mary said, "we also can't suppose that just because a person is a stranger to us, their motive is greed."

"As in they have their own heartaches and needs."

"Exactly," Mary said.

Betty laughed lightly. "I think I need breakfast. This is a lot to ponder this early in the morning. My brain needs carbs. How about pancakes? I found some blueberries in the freezer." She moved slowly to the freezer, and Mary could tell her arthritis was bothering her.

"That sounds heavenly," Mary said and went over to the counter to help Betty mix the ingredients.

"Do you have any suspects? Have you started a list?"

Mary cracked an egg into a bowl, her brow furrowed. "Putting aside motive—whether greed or compassion—Nigel Finnian is at the top of my list. I hate to say it, but Heidi Gilbert is on the list too, mainly because of where she was standing when we closed. Plus, she was talking vaguely about her financial struggles and about how too many people live in the Gilberts' house."

"Okay, so far you've got Nigel Finnian and Heidi Gilbert. Anyone else?"

"Bob Hiller." She swallowed hard. "Though I can hardly bear to think about it."

Later that morning, when Mary pulled up to the Chickadee Inn, a light cloud cover was blowing in from the Atlantic, and the air had turned chilly.

Two vehicles were parked in the driveway, a large luxury SUV—apparently a guest's—and the owner's small white van with Chickadee Inn logos on the side doors. She parked near the entrance and gazed up at the buttercup-yellow two-story building. It was a mix of Cape Cod and Victorian, with white gingerbread trim and an accent of forest green.

Alexa came to the door almost before Mary could ring the bell. "Come in, come in," she said, taking a few steps backward. "It's looking colder and cloudier by the minute." She smiled. "It's good to see you again."

Mary stepped inside. "Thanks so much. Betty's thrilled to be helping you decorate. And from what I can tell, things are already looking beautiful."

"Aren't they? Betty is just the woman for the job." She gestured toward a daintily decorated front parlor with floral upholstered furniture and views of the bay. "I bought the place 'as is,' and everything is certainly workable. But my tastes are a bit more, well, shall we say 'sophisticated' than the previous owner." She smiled, raising her chin a bit. "I like a more traditional look, rather than frilly. Something more in keeping with Cape Cod." She stopped abruptly and smiled. "Would you like a tour?"

Mary grinned. "I'd love one."

As Mary followed Alexa upstairs, Alexa turned to look down as she spoke. "We're a relatively small bed-and-breakfast, eight guest rooms, all upstairs." She stopped at the top and waited for Mary to join her.

She continued speaking as they walked down the hall, which was covered with a floral wallpaper in pinks and pale greens. Across the top was a border that appeared to be stenciled with the same motif, though larger. At the far end of the hall was a large window covered with ceiling-to-floor ivory lace swag curtains.

"So eighties," Alexa said with a sniff. "I have an idea for the direction I'd like to go with the whole inn, but I thought it best to have Betty begin with a guest room first to see if what I've dreamed up in my head works in reality." She laughed and opened the last door on the left.

Mary peeked in. "Ah, so this is the work in progress." She blinked. Betty had her work cut out for her. Alexa apparently had workmen remove the old wallpaper and prep the wall for new paper or paint. She turned back to Alexa. "You're very wise to start small."

Alexa laughed. "I can't imagine waking up to an entire redecorating scheme that you dislike, but it's too late to change." She closed the door, and Mary followed her back down the stairs to the wide entry.

Alexa gestured widely. "The rest you've mostly seen."

Beyond the large entry—where Alexa kept a burled wood desk for check-ins, a small file to one side, and a laptop computer behind—was the floral tearoom Mary had seen earlier. On the opposite side of the entry was a comfortable-looking, less frilly game and reading room. An antique hand-carved chess table took up the space at one end, a piano at the other. Near the fireplace was a grouping of chairs for visiting or reading.

"Let's sit for a moment in the tearoom," Alexa said and led Mary back through the entry toward the room where they'd started the tour. As Mary settled into a love seat–sized settee, Alexa sat in a high-back chair across from her and folded her delicate hands in her lap. "I can't imagine that you stopped by for a tour, though it's been pleasant to show you my little pride and joy." She hesitated, still smiling. "Was there another reason that prompted your visit? Is there something I can help you with?"

Mary drew in a deep breath. "Yes, there is. I have a question about the time of arrival of one of your guests."

"I'm sorry, Mary, but I keep all information confidential," Alexa said, her smile fading. "Even such obscure things as arrival times. I'm sure you understand."

"Completely." Mary hadn't expected this would be easy, and she respected Alexa's stern policy. But she continued to press just a little harder, Isabella's image securely in her mind. "But I'm investigating something that happened in my shop— something has disappeared—and I'm collecting as much information as I can. I can't be sure, but it may have something to do with one of your guests."

Alexa's expression changed as her eyes darkened. "What was it that disappeared?"

"I wish I could say, but I'm not"—Mary tried to think of a gracious way to avoid answering the question—"really at liberty. I can only tell you that it's important. Very important."

"Valuable?" Alexa quirked a brow. Mary wondered if she'd heard the rumors about the book and its "million dollar" value.

"Very valuable," Mary said, hoping the urgency she was portraying would help convince Alexa to help her.

"I can see from your expression that it has greater value than something simply with a price tag fixed on it."

Mary let out a breath. "That's exactly right." But the sense of relief was quickly followed by mild alarm: How could Alexa have known? Was it a lucky guess? Or did Mary's expression really show her feelings to that extent?

Mary smiled to put her at ease. "That's why I'd hoped to find out if any of your guests were delayed by the bridge being out the night of the storm." Every detail mattered, especially who arrived when, and who might or might not have been telling the truth about their arrival time. Could one of the book chat participants have been lying about when they'd arrived? The idea nagged at her. "I am not asking for names, only the times."

Alexa hesitated just long enough for Mary to see that she knew more than she was saying. Otherwise, why would the arrival time of one or two unidentified guests be important to keep confidential? "As I said, all information about my guests is confidential. Besides," she went on, "I would assume there are agencies where you can get information about the bridge."

"I understand," Mary said, seeing that the woman was obviously not going to budge. She was about to stand to leave when the tea Betty had suggested came to mind. And truth be known, she was now more curious about Alexa than ever. "On a happy note," she said, "Betty suggested the three of us have tea together, and I thought it was a great idea. I'd love to get to know you better."

Alexa's eyes brightened. "I'd love that too," she said. "And, of course, I'll be happy to host here. How about Friday afternoon?"

Mary smiled warmly. "That sounds perfect. I'll double-check with Betty." A new thought occurred. "By the way, do you happen to know when the bridge went out the other night and how long it took the crews to get traffic moving again?"

"I can answer that," said a voice behind her.

Mary turned to see a statuesque redhead descending the stairs. "I was caught in the mess. Traffic was backed up for miles. It was a nightmare. One literally couldn't go anywhere." Mary fought to keep her jaw from dropping. The woman, dressed in a pale sea-foam-green pants outfit, wearing high-heeled boots trimmed in what appeared to be real mink, walked toward her. She was runway-model stunning and wore a beautiful cameo necklace at her neck.

"Mary Fisher," Alexa said to the woman and then turned to Mary. "Mary, meet my newest guest..." Alexa flushed, obviously unwilling to give away the guest's name. Apparently even that was confidential.

The woman smiled and extended her hand. "Ms. Laurie Block," she finished for Alexa. "The Bourne Bridge," Ms. Block said, "on my route, at least, was out for more than twelve hours. I heard the Sagamore Bridge was out even longer. The ferries weren't operating because of the high waves. I was quite afraid I would freeze to death before they got it cleared enough to reroute the traffic."

"What time did the worst of it hit?" Mary asked.

"Long before I got there," Ms. Block said. "I should have checked, I suppose, before I left Weston. So I have only myself to blame, I suppose."

"Weston?" Mary said.

Ms. Block tilted her head and frowned. "Yes, Weston, why?"

"Oh, nothing," she said, trying to think fast, her heart beating a little faster. Orris Rathburn's office was in Weston, a small town west of Boston where, very likely, people knew one another's business. Mary knew that it boasted homes worth millions but a very small population. Coincidence?

She gathered her wits as quickly as she could, thanked Laurie, started for the door, then hesitated and turned.

"Laurie, do you happen to know a man here in town named Nigel Finnian?"

Alexa frowned briefly as if confused. But it was Ms. Block's expression that captured her attention.

Was it her imagination, or did Ms. Block's eyes flicker with recognition? If so, she quickly recovered. "No," she said calmly. "Why?"

Mary smiled and shook her head. "Oh, just curious. I believe he has a friend staying here and just wasn't sure if it was you."

Ms. Block laughed lightly and waved her fingers. "I'll be here indefinitely, so it's not a tragedy if I missed someone who's trying to find me." She laughed again.

Mary wrapped her scarf around her neck, puzzled at the woman's strange response. "It's a pleasure to meet you, Laurie, and I look forward to seeing you on Friday, Alexa."

As she drove off, questions flew into her head one after another. Was Orris connected to this woman? And was Ms. Block the person Nigel Finnian was looking for when Mary followed him here? And was her "indefinite stay" something she wanted to get back to one or the other? Or both?

If so, why?

Could Orris have found another buyer who would pay more money? With the original bid accepted, was it too late to back out of the deal with the first? So did he hire this team—Laurie and Nigel—to steal it from her shop? Perhaps Orris knew Laurie and told her, and she somehow enlisted Nigel's help. Or perhaps Mary's imagination was running away with her.

Still, she couldn't ignore the thought. Was Orris another suspect on her list?

She turned on Main Street toward her bookshop. She'd told Orris about Isabella, and he'd listened to her joy over being able to help the child and her family with the proceeds from the sale.

She believed the best about people until they proved her wrong. She hoped above all hope her theory was wrong about Orris Rathburn.

TEN

Mary stepped out of her car in front of the bookshop. Though the day was chilly, a sprinkle of shoppers were scattered along the sidewalks of Main Street. Despite her mind being occupied by her encounter with Alexa and Laurie, she was still struck, as she often was, by the quaint storefronts around her. They reminded her of scenes from a storybook, perhaps even a little town with a Robert Louis Stevenson's "Counterpane" look to it. This was one of those times, maybe because of the pleasant faces and smiles as people strolled along the street.

Henry pulled up in his 1953 Chevy Bel Air. The convertible top was up, and for good reason. He started to head into the Black & White Diner across the street, then spotted Mary and strode in her direction.

His face lit up when he stopped in front of her on the sidewalk. "Well, look here. Now it's an even better day than I thought it would be," he said, his smile widening. "I was hoping I'd run into you."

Mary felt the warmth of a blush and laughed.

His smile disappeared as he studied her face. "What's going on? Are you okay?"

Mary shook her head. "Is it that obvious?"

"Something's on your mind, that's for sure," Henry said, his distinct New England accent expressing his concern.

Mary knew she could trust Henry above almost anyone, so she quickly and quietly relayed the news about the missing book to him. She told him about what she'd learned so far, and who she was considering as suspects. It felt good to share the details with him, especially knowing that he was a consistently helpful brainstormer.

"How about Chief McArthur? Has he discovered anything?"

"No, nothing." She told him about following the BMW to the bed-and-breakfast, her conversation with Alexa and then with Ms. Block. She drew in a deep breath. "And then there's this Weston connection..."

"The town?"

"Yes. That's where Laurie Block lives, apparently. That's also where Orris's business address is."

"Could be a coincidence."

She grinned. "My thinking exactly. But it just seems *too* coincidental, considering recent events."

"Do I see a Google bubble over your head?"

Mary laughed at the comic-strip reference. "As soon as I can get to it."

Henry's expression grew sober. "Well, if you ever need help, you just holler. No matter where or when."

"Thank you, Henry. You're a good friend."

He smiled and touched his forehead in a mock salute.

As Mary unlocked the door to Mary's Bookshop, Henry started to walk away. Then he turned and strode back. "Mary, I know you're a strong and capable woman, but—"

Mary put her hand on Henry's forearm. "I know you're about to tell me to be careful, and believe me, I will, Henry. I promise."

Mary stepped inside the shop, turned on the lights, and had just taken her place behind the counter, when her first customers came in. As they browsed, she eased into the chair in front of her computer, powered it on, and waited to be asked for her password.

She could hear the customers, all locals, happily chatting about the latest best sellers.

Before she could type in her password, Mason Willoughby, owner of a local art gallery, came over to make a purchase, asking Mary if she planned to hold another book chat. "I'm a big Agatha Christie fan but couldn't make the chat the other night," he explained. "I wanted to finish a painting I was working on . . . at least I'd planned to until the lights went out. Will there be another chat?"

"Absolutely," she said, smiling. "Same time, same place."

She stopped to think about what she'd said and almost did an air punch the way she'd seen her grandchildren do. Of course! Another book chat was exactly the ticket. She grinned as she laid out a plan in her mind. All the culprits would gather in the same room in which the crime had taken place. How many mystery writers used such a ploy to find their culprit? Exact circumstances would be repeated down to the finest detail. Mary hoped that then the gradual unveiling of the truth would happen.

But many things would need to be lined up. She grinned. Get her ducks lined up in a row, as some might say. And she had only four days to do it. She pulled out a pad and began to draft her plan. Yes. Miss Marple had done it. Jessica Fletcher had done it. Mary Fisher would do it too.

A few of the customers left, and the others seemed content to browse. Two preschoolers played in the children's corner, and an older woman asked if the teapots were for sale. Mary glanced at the clock.

Just as she wondered why Rebecca was late, her cell phone rang. She checked the ID. It was Rebecca.

"I'm so sorry we're running late this morning," Rebecca said. "Aunt Millicent wanted to drop some things by Heidi's. They got to talking, and"—she laughed lightly—"well, I had a terrible time getting Aunt Millicent back in the car. But we're on our way."

"That's fine," Mary said. "I do have some errands to run later, but they can wait."

"Is it all right if Aunt Millicent comes with me again?"

"Of course." She chuckled. "She was truly a pleasure to have in the shop."

"We'll be there in half a jiffy," Rebecca said.

Mary helped two more customers, then turned back to the computer. First, she typed in Laurie Block. Several women with Facebook accounts came up, a couple of California Realtors by that name, and a romance author. But none of their photos matched the woman Mary had met at the bed-and-breakfast.

Next, she typed in Nigel Finnian.

She expected a hit on that one, but she sat back, astounded at the pages and pages of links to his name.

She clicked on the first, a newspaper account that covered a controversial trial in Boston in which he was the defending attorney.

She'd only read partway through the rather tedious account when Rebecca and Millicent came in the back door.

Millicent's face lit up when she spotted the rocker, which Mary had purposefully left by the fireplace. But before sitting down, she came over to Mary, her jeweled cane tapping, and stopped in front of her.

"Thank you for making me feel at home," she said. "Remember what I said about helping you out. If there's anything I can do…" She raised a silver eyebrow. "I've got more get-up-and-go than you might think."

"Thank you," Mary said gently. "I'll remember that."

"I'm a pretty good sleuth too," she said with a knowing wink. "Should you be in need of one." She patted her tote. "Have you ever read any of the Seaside Knitters mysteries? I've read them all, which makes me something of an expert."

"I'll keep that in mind," Mary said with genuine kindness. But then she realized she hadn't told Millicent about the missing book. Had Rebecca? Or had she overheard Mary talking with Heidi? "Millicent, out of curiosity, how did you hear about the theft?"

"Oh, Rebecca told me," she said. "I hope that's okay. I sensed a bit of tension from you yesterday, and I was praying for you all day from my place on the rocker. I asked Rebecca about it when we got home. You must be so disappointed. And that poor little girl."

Millicent's empathy made Mary almost want to cry; the woman felt genuinely bad for the loss of the book. "I am disappointed, that's for sure. But I'm still hoping to recover the book and help Isabella."

"I'm sure you will," Millicent said, then lowered her head and pulled out her crocheting materials.

Mary went back to the computer screen to see what else she could find out about Nigel Finnian.

She clicked on the next news account, this time a tabloid newspaper masquerading as a society page. As she read, her eyes widened. She bent closer, scanning from one side of the screen to the other, her heart quickening as she took in the news account.

He was a collector of rare books.

He was also having marital problems, and word had it his wife had kicked him out. He had disappeared from the Boston scene, and no one knew where he'd gone.

His wife had issued a two-word response to the reporter's query: "No comment."

It was time to start asking some questions of Mr. Finnian.

"Can you watch the shop for me?" Mary called to Rebecca who was in the back room.

Rebecca poked her head around the corner. "You got it."

"I don't know how long I'll be."

"Take your time," Rebecca said.

"We'll take care of the shop," Millicent said. "Don't you worry for a minute."

Mary grinned at the older woman. She was still curious about Millicent's sleuthing comment, but the woman's earnestness made Mary smile. She wondered how long she planned to stay with her niece. If she was this comfortable after just a few days, she might want to run the shop after a few weeks.

Laughing to herself, Mary got into the Impala and pulled out into the street.

———

A few minutes later, Mary parked her car near the cluster of fishing shanties near the dunes, where the address Nigel had given Bob was located. She would have normally walked there, but with the weather the way it was, she much preferred taking her car.

Weathered and desolate, the shanties held their own kind of enchantment and were a far cry from the famous Cape Cod beauties on the far side of the bay. If she weren't so focused on Nigel Finnian and her determination to find out everything she could about him, Mary would have wanted to walk along the beach and look out at the bay waters she loved.

She whispered a prayer and gathered up her courage, checked her notebook again for the address, and then locked her purse in the trunk of the car. She quickly pulled on her coat and started out across the sand toward the shanties. Her boots crunched in the mix of sand and ice.

The cold wind had kicked up again, and streaks of clouds crossed the sky. As she walked across the dunes, the mix of sand and tiny particles of ice, blown by the wind, covered her footprints within seconds.

She was within yards of the first cabin, which was obviously deserted, when she noticed that smoke rose from the chimney of the third one down. A man sat in an Adirondack chair in the sand several yards from the shanty. It appeared to be Nigel Finnian.

He was bundled in a heavy parka and stocking cap, and dozens of loose papers whirled in the wind above him and blew along the sand around him.

He seemed oblivious and was eerily still. Was he all right?

ELEVEN

---◆◆◆---

Two dark eyes, closed just a moment ago, now looked up at Mary, confused. Nigel sat up, rubbed his eyes, and looked around.

Then he peered up into her face. "There's a glare from the water behind you. Would you mind coming around where I can see who you are?"

"I'm sorry I woke you," Mary said and stepped around where he could get a better look. "I'm Mary Fisher. We met the other night at my bookshop."

Finally, a smile crept across his face. "Of course," he said and tried to stand.

He pulled off his cap and rubbed his hair, making him appear even more unkempt than the day before. He now had another day's growth added to his chin stubble.

He looked up at the sky, out to the bay, and closer in at the dunes, still being sculpted by the wind. He let out a sigh, deep and heavy. "Wouldn't you know it," he said, his voice still gravelly, "my manuscript...flying from here to kingdom come?" He stood and halfheartedly began snatching at the loose papers.

"I'll help." Mary moved across the dunes, grabbing the papers as she walked. They were strewn so far down the beach that she wondered if they might end up at the lighthouse.

The wind was picking up now, more frigid than ever, and she didn't hear Nigel come up behind her. "Please," he said, "there's really no need for you to do this. It was my fault I fell asleep with the manuscript in my lap. I've got a copy on my laptop anyway. Not much has been lost."

"You're writing a book?" Mary reached to grab another airborne sheet.

He laughed, though without humor. "A novel," he said. "The great American novel," he added with self-effacing sarcasm.

She stopped and stared at him. "That's why you've come to Ivy Bay? To work on your novel?"

Again, he laughed. Again, deadpan. "Among other reasons."

Mary drew in a breath and then looked down at the manuscript page in her left hand. At the top was printed page 107. It was neatly double-spaced and in Courier font. It looked completely legit. But just because he was a writer wanting to publish a book didn't mean he couldn't also be a thief.

No matter what she thought about his down-and-out appearance, his air of defeat, or whether or not the tabloid account about his rare-book collecting and downward spiral was true, her first priority was to find the missing book.

She had questions to ask, but needed answers, not evasions. She sent a quick prayer heavenward that she might proceed with wisdom.

He stared at her, holding the mess of papers in his arms. His eyes seemed to have sunk into their sockets. He rubbed his hair and jammed the cap back onto his head and then turned to leave.

"Are you running from something, Mr. Finnian?"

He turned and looked at her in surprise. "That's an odd question."

"Or hiding something?" she pressed.

He stared at her. "Such as...?"

"I hear you're a rare-book collector."

"So, you've been reading up on me. May I ask why?"

Mary nibbled her lip, wondering how much she should give away in this line of questioning. He was her prime suspect, but she didn't want to outright accuse him quite yet. He might bolt, and she would never see the book again.

"The night you were in my shop," she said, "something of value disappeared."

He looked up sharply, his eyes narrowing. "That's why you're here? You think I stole something from you?" He tilted his head toward the sky, and his shoulders began to shake. "That's classic. Just classic." He was laughing, as if at the heavens.

"I gave you my card, and I suppose a Google search followed." He gestured toward the shanty. "And suddenly, all this looks like I'm hiding something. Or hiding from the law."

Mary drew in a sharp breath, wondering what she'd missed in the rest of the articles listed on the pages that came up on her Internet search. "Well, actually, yes, it does."

His eyes turned dark. "Well, Mary, I guess you'll take this at face value. I'm here to work on a lifelong dream, write a novel. If I'm hiding from anything, it's myself." That last sentence he said as if to himself, quiet and distracted.

She was getting nowhere. "Okay," she said.

He started to walk away from her, but she hurried through the blowing sand to catch up. "Look, Mr. Finnian. There's a child who needs medical care. The missing item was to be sold to help the little girl and her family. If you did have anything to do with the missing item, please...please know that a little girl's safety is on the line."

She had his full attention, and she noticed for the first time the mask was gone, that mask she noticed the first night where his smile didn't reach his eyes.

"I'm so sorry," he said, and with a dejected wave, he trudged on to the shanty.

Mary watched his sloped shoulders as he walked up the weathered steps to the door.

He said he was sorry. Was it a confession of some sort?

Mary didn't know what to think at this point. She closed her eyes for a moment, wanting to follow. If he *did* have the book in his possession, what if he'd hidden it right there in the shanty, just yards from where she stood?

She pictured Isabella in her hospital bed, pictured herself pounding on the shanty door and demanding that Nigel give her some straight answers.

She smiled as she headed back to her car. You catch more bees with honey than with vinegar. She would come back, and next time, she would bring him a batch of Betty's cookies.

She was halfway to the car when another question came to her. And it couldn't wait for her to return with chocolate-chip cookies.

She trotted to the shanty once more, climbed the worn steps, and knocked.

A weary-looking Nigel Finnian opened the door. He let out a deep sigh. "I'm beginning to think I've run into the ghost of Columbo."

She couldn't help laughing. "Not many young people remember him."

He didn't laugh with her. "What is it?"

"Are you missing a comb?"

"What?"

"An antique-looking man's comb. Perhaps from early in the last century."

He stared at her. "You came all the way back here to ask me that? Or were you sitting out there in the sand trying to come up with something new to ask me?"

"The comb, Mr. Finnian," she reminded him. "Is yours missing?"

"No," he said and then gave her a mirthless laugh and shut the door in her face.

TWELVE

A storm blew in off the Atlantic during the night, and by morning, the rain and sleet had turned into a powdery snow that caught the wind and piled against the shops on Main Street. The roads were plowed and salted but remained treacherous. Mary slowed her car to a crawl, feeling the wheels crunch through the ice. Her windshield wipers beat back and forth, wiping away the light snow that still fell. Inside, her defroster tried to keep up with the window fog, but even so, every few minutes, she rubbed the glass with her gloved hand.

Within a few minutes, she was on Meeting House Road and spotted the Little Neck Pharmacy up ahead, cautiously signaled, and moved to the right so she could turn into the parking lot. Betty's rheumatoid arthritis was acting up that morning, so her sister asked Mary to stop by the pharmacy for her medication before going in to the bookshop.

Mary parked and then held her breath as she opened the car door and the frigid air hit her. Bundled in a down full-length coat, her neck wrapped in a woolen scarf long enough to draw over her head, she gingerly made her way through the snow drifts into the drugstore.

She stomped the snow off her boots and then headed to the pharmacy at the back, soles squeaking with each step.

Jacob Ames, pharmacist and owner of the pharmacy that had been in the Ames family for years, gave Mary a smile when he saw her at the counter. Mary didn't know when she'd ever seen him when he didn't have a prickly look beneath his balding comb-over, especially when he had a rush of customers during the summer season. "My first customer," he said. "Maybe my only customer on a day like today." He added a grumpy sniff for emphasis. "What can I get you?"

Betty had called ahead for her refill, and Jacob went to a shelf behind the counter to retrieve it. Mary heard the door open and more customers enter the drugstore, teeth chattering as they talked about the cold. Jacob was officially wrong about Mary being the only customer of the day.

The interior was small, and voices carried. Two women, as bundled up as she was, drifted toward the pharmacy and stood in line behind her. She didn't recognize their voices, but before she could turn to see who was speaking, Jacob returned with the medication and rang it up on the cash register.

As she waited for change, a woman with a hushed tone said, "I have to say I'm surprised. Poor Mrs. Gilbert is beside herself with worry. She doesn't know where the kids got the money for the house. I mean, she already resents the fact that they got married so young, then had to move in with them, and then Heidi ups and gets pregnant. With twins, of all things." Mary was suddenly on high alert.

The second person tsk-tsked, and then the woman with the quiet voice went on. "And anyway, where would they get that kind of cash?"

"Maybe it's wishful thinking on the kids' part," the second woman said.

"Yeah, maybe. You know how kids can be these days. 'We know you love having us here, Mom. Just think how bad you'll feel when we move out.' You know, that sort of thing. Wanting Mom and Dad to beg them to stay."

"It's been known to happen," the second voice said at the same time Jacob Ames was going over the instructions for the medication with Mary.

Mary put the medication into her handbag, ducked into her woolen scarf, and headed for the exit.

———

When Mary arrived at the bookshop a little before nine, her mind was still focused on the gossip she'd just heard about Heidi. She couldn't deny the connection the subject matter had to her missing book, and if it was true, it kept Heidi steadily on her suspect list. A young woman, in need of cash, suddenly buys a home. The women in the pharmacy had wondered where Heidi had come up with the money. Mary was afraid she might know the answer.

She sighed and looked out the large paneled window by the front counter, and watched as the sun tried to peek out from the still-heavy-laden storm clouds. Bars of sunlight dotted the little town. The shallow drifts of snow sparkled against the red-brick buildings with their peaked icicle-ringed roofs, and windows glowed from inside as shopkeepers turned over their Welcome signs. Only a few brave souls strolled along the sidewalks, and most were walking dogs that looked floppy-eared happy to be outdoors, snuffling the drifts and finding places to do their business. The scene brought a much-needed dose of encouragement to her heart.

Rebecca wouldn't be in for a while. Mary placed Gus's carrier on the floor and opened it. He jumped out and rubbed up against Mary's legs. She stooped and gave him a rub behind his ears. His answering purr made her smile.

"Hey, buddy, it's cold in here." She went over to the fireplace, Gus at her heels, and quickly turned on the gas logs and put on water for tea. Then, unwinding her scarf and doffing her coat, she placed it on the coatrack in the back room.

The phone rang, and she caught it on the fourth ring. "Mary's Mystery Bookshop," she said breathlessly. She sat on the stool near the cash register and picked up a pen.

"This is the *Boston Globe*," a young female voice said. "Please hold for our reporter...."

Mary blinked in surprise. "Who?"

But canned music played in her ear. She was on hold and didn't even want to be on the phone. But she also didn't want to be rude, so she waited.

Gus jumped up on the counter and sat down on her notepad.

A young woman finally came on the line. "We understand that a very rare and valuable book—*The Murder of Roger Ackroyd* by Agatha Christie—is missing from your bookshop. Can you tell us if that's true?"

Had it really gotten this far? Mary nibbled her bottom lip. Now she really didn't want to speak to the reporter. "I'm sorry, but I really can't comment," Mary said, though not unkindly.

"Word has it that it's worth $100,000."

Mary couldn't help laughing. A hundred thousand? At least this was less than the million-dollar figure Bob Hiller had given her.

At Mary's chuckle, the woman pressed on. "If not $100,000, can you tell us how much it is worth?"

Mary sighed, kept her voice kind and again said, "No comment."

Mary finally ended the call, and for a moment, petted Gus, thinking through the connection between the call from Boston and how the word might have come to the attention of the reporter. Then before putting down her phone, she punched in another number.

"Orris Rathburn and Associates," a deep voice said after a few rings. "Rathburn here."

"Mr. Rathburn, this is Mary Fisher."

"Of course, Mary. It's good to hear from you. Have you heard anything about the book? The local police department apparently heard from your chief, and they're running a concurrent investigation on this end." He sighed heavily and then added, "I'm sorry. I didn't give you a chance to answer my question. I do have a tendency to do that. My wife complains about it a lot." He paused. "Let me start over. Have you heard anything about our missing *Roger Ackroyd*?"

She smiled at the quirk. "No, I haven't. I know our chief will leave no stone unturned, but I've heard nothing yet. I'm investigating on my own but haven't discovered anything."

"I hear from friends in Ivy Bay that you've got quite a reputation for solving mysteries."

Mary felt herself blush. "I've just been lucky, I suppose."
A better word was *blessed*. She didn't believe in luck. "The
reason I called is to find out if you know anything about a
reporter from the *Boston Globe* doing an investigation."

"No, not a thing. They haven't contacted us for a statement
or anything. Did they contact you?"

"Yes. I just now got a call. They'd heard the book was
worth $100,000. But I didn't give her any other information."

"Probably wise," Orris said.

"What I can't figure out is how such high numbers have
begun to circulate."

"You know how things get exaggerated," he said.

A moment of silence fell between them, and Mary again
wondered if another buyer had made such an offer. What if
that rumor had some basis for truth? The dollar amount was
outrageous, but it wouldn't be the first time a determined
buyer, for personal reasons, made an outrageous offer on an
item.

"Mr. Rathburn, did any other offers come in after we
accepted the initial one?" She held her breath, waiting for an
answer.

He chuckled. "Yes, actually, there were a few—but
they came in after I'd agreed to the terms of the first
offer. Contractually, legally, we were bound to sell to the
representatives of the first bid we accepted."

"Were any as high as $100,000?"

He laughed. "No, not even close. That's the rumor mill
for you. It seems this is a very popular book that collectors
have been searching for for years. Even I was surprised. They
were all disappointed when I told them it had sold."

"Word does get around," Mary said.

"Yes, doesn't it? Listen, I have another call coming in. Can you hold?"

"Yes."

Mary sat pondering all he'd said, but the question about an association with Nigel Finnian kept running through her mind. When he came back on the line, she took a deep breath.

"I've met someone I think is a rare-book collector from Weston. At least that's what a newspaper account on the Internet said about him."

"I may know him. Weston's not that big a town."

"That's what I was thinking," she said easily. "He's vacationing here on the bay and visited our shop the night the book was taken."

There was a moment of silence. Then Orris said, "Really. Very interesting. What's this collector's name?"

"Nigel Finnian."

"Oh yes, Finnian."

She sat up straight, now on full alert.

"I don't really know him, just of him. He's a trial lawyer in Boston, handles high-profile cases. In the local papers a lot. Society page info mostly. We don't go out socially, we're not friends, but we do belong to the same country club and do see each other from time to time. Very casual. He lives here in Weston, but he spends most of his time at his firm in Boston."

Mary sighed and leaned back. She wanted to believe that Orris was telling the truth, but he did seem rather quick with abundant details about how the two were only acquaintances. Was Orris being honest, or were he and Nigel working together and trying to confuse her?

THIRTEEN

—◆◆◆—

Mary went to the computer and again typed in Nigel Finnian. Just as her previous search, several references popped up within seconds.

She bypassed the first two sites she'd read the previous day.

She clicked on the link to the next reference, which took her to the Web site of his firm. Orris was correct. Finnian handled high-profile, one might even say, glitzy cases. His profile photo looked like the man who'd first entered her shop the night of the theft, but nothing like the man she'd seen at the shanty.

She sat back, staring at the computer monitor, and then clicked on the next link, a society page article that featured Finnian.

Then she clicked on another. And another. With each, she leaned forward with great interest. He and his brunette wife were among the social elite of Boston, to be sure. There were photos of them attending plays, the opera, parties, fund-raisers, political events... the references went on for pages.

She clicked on one of the most recent. There was Nigel, looking much as he had the night of his arrival. His suit was of an expensive cut, his haircut perfect, his jawline clean-shaven, and his expression more sure of himself than arrogant.

The woman by his side was a brown-eyed, brunette beauty. Shorter than Nigel by a foot, she held herself with grace and elegance, her dark eyes sparkling as she beamed proudly up at her husband.

Mary zoomed in on the photo, enlarging it to the size of the computer screen. She focused on the shape of the jawline, the small cleft in the perfectly cut chin, the wide beautifully shaped eyes.

But there was something about her... something familiar she couldn't shake. She zoomed in a bit more.

The guest dressed in sea-foam green at Alexa's bed-and-breakfast came to mind, though she had nothing in common physically with the woman in the photo. Or did she?

Different eye color, but that was easy enough to change. Same with the hair color. Same verdict. Wigs were an option.

Height? The woman in the photo seemed shorter, though she couldn't tell for certain.

She stared at the photo, clicked on a few more, then came back to the original and zoomed in yet closer for a better look. Were her eyes deceiving her?

She was wearing a cameo necklace that looked very similar to the one worn by Laurie Block.

She needed to get a closer look at the woman at Chickadee Inn. Her heartbeat quickened. What if she had the book with her, right under Alexa's nose, right under Betty's, and even Mary's when Alexa gave Mary the tour?

She nibbled her bottom lip as she settled back in her chair for a moment, playing with ideas for arranging a meeting with the woman she now believed was Mrs. Nigel Finnian. There was the tea at the Chickadee the following day, but she couldn't be guaranteed Mrs. Finnian would be there. Besides, this couldn't wait.

But she also needed to be armed with as much information as she could gather.

She leaned forward and scanned a few more articles and photos, including one that featured Nigel's love of collecting rare, irreplaceable books, and he almost jokingly mentioned he'd once tried his hand at writing but had given it up because his law practice took too much time.

Then came a terse statement issued by Nigel's law office that said Nigel found it necessary after the breakup of his marriage to keep a low profile, indicating that he was backing out of the social scene and taking some time off. The reporter asked about Mrs. Finnian and her accusations of infidelity, and Nigel simply answered, "No comment."

Was this a reason Mrs. Finnian aka Ms. Laurie Block might dress in disguise? If it was indeed her, had she come to Ivy Bay to spy on her husband? Or was it part of a big hoax that provided a cover for them both to carry out the heist? Why else was Nigel expecting his wife (if that was who he'd asked Alexa about) the previous day?

She sat back again, pondering the clues she'd just been handed via the Internet. Yes, they were dots. She sighed deeply. She just couldn't get them to connect.

And these dots seemed to be coming at her faster than she could keep up. Her mind went back to the rumor she'd overheard at the pharmacy about Heidi and her husband, Cade. More dots. Perhaps connected. Perhaps not.

Either way, she had to find out if there was any truth to the tidbit of gossip.

But first things first. As soon as Rebecca arrived, she would head to the bed-and-breakfast for another visit, this time she hoped with the woman she strongly suspected was Nigel Finnian's soon-to-be ex-wife.

Mary was gathering her purse and coat when Rebecca and Millicent came in, shivering from the cold.

"This is weather for penguins," Millicent said as she headed to the fireplace and her favorite chair. She set her yarn tote on the floor, rubbed her hands together in front of the fire, and then turned to Mary, flexing her swollen fingers. "My arthritis kicks up something fierce during this kind of weather. It makes it hard to crochet, and I have some beautiful projects started. They'll have to wait, I suppose."

Mary met Rebecca's eyes and noticed how utterly weary she looked. She wondered how long Aunt Millicent's visit would turn out to be. Already, it seemed to be taking its toll.

Her heart went out to Rebecca. Her great-aunt had been her constant shadow all week. It struck her that as much as her employee loved Millicent, she might enjoy some time without her. It wouldn't hurt to change the order of her investigation. After all, when she met Ms. Laurie Block, she'd said she would be in Ivy Bay indefinitely.

She looked at Millicent. "I need to go out to visit Heidi. Would you like to go with me?"

"Would I?" Millicent had gathered her tote and cane almost before the words were out of Mary's mouth.

Mary glanced at Rebecca whose eyes lit up immediately. She grinned and mouthed, "Thank you."

They settled into the car, the heater blasting, and Millicent settled back in the seat, smiling as if in heaven. "Thank you for inviting me," she said. "I like that young woman." She placed her handbag on her lap, her hands folded on top. She was so short she didn't seem able to see over the dashboard. After a few minutes, they pulled up to the double-wide trailer. This was the first time Mary had seen it in daylight, and her heart sank as she took in the conditions.

Tools were strewn around the carport, just as before, but this time, two older cars sat in the driveway, hoods up, with parts scattered here and there. Another vehicle, a pickup, under a snow-covered awning nearby. A Christmas tree, long past its prime, was lying on its side on the front porch. A rusted tricycle had been tossed topsy-turvy next to it. Several plastic pots were stacked by the front door.

"Heidi told me her husband repairs cars to bring in extra money," Millicent said. "But this is such a pitiful sight. Just pitiful." She drew in a trembling sigh.

Mary parked close to a wide spot on the asphalt that wasn't snow or ice covered, got out, and went around to help Millicent.

When she knocked, it took a few minutes before the sound of footsteps carried toward them from the other side of the door.

A woman opened the door. Behind her, Mary could see a dimly lit room with very little furniture. And it was cold. Extremely cold inside. They obviously had no heat. The woman had a blanket wrapped around her, and judging from the bulges, a coat underneath that. She looked at Mary expectantly.

Mary realized that she had been too stunned to speak.

"Yes?" The woman said. "May I help you?"

"I'm looking for Heidi Gilbert," Mary said. She hadn't expected the poverty that was in front of her. "I'm Mary Fisher, and this is my friend Millicent Quilp."

"I've heard a lot about you," she said, looking at Millicent who gave her a beaming smile.

Then she turned back to Mary. "I'm Sharon Gilbert," she said and then added, "Come in." She stepped back and opened the door wider.

Mary and Millicent stepped inside. "Please, sit down," Sharon said. "My husband's at work, Cade's in school, and Heidi—" She shrugged. "Who knows where Heidi is. The girl beats to her own drum." Sharon gave a polite smile, but Mary could tell the woman was annoyed with Heidi. "Not that I blame her. There are four of us living in this tiny place, and now we've got Cade's twins on the way...." Her voice trailed off.

Mary looked around, hoping the rumor was true. That the family was indeed going to be moving to a better place.

She only hoped it wasn't because of the stolen book.

But how else could it be?

Sharon reached for a tissue and blew her nose, and Mary realized she had started crying. "I'm sorry, I'm a terrible host.

I'm not usually this emotional. It's just that Heidi and I have been arguing about...Never mind. You certainly didn't come here to talk about this." The woman straightened her spine and raised her chin. "How can I help you?"

"It's okay," Mary said. "We came at a bad time—"

But Millicent cut in. "No, no. Dear woman. What's the matter? How can we help *you*?"

Mrs. Gilbert looked at Millicent with an almost childlike plea, as if Millicent's offer was just what she'd needed. "Do you know what she had the audacity to suggest?"

Mary had the feeling she knew what was coming, and she held her breath. She exchanged a glance with Millicent, whose compassionate expression softened Mary's own. She turned her apt attention to Heidi's mother-in-law.

"Supposedly, she and Cade have 'found' enough money to make a down payment on a house—a real house—for us all to live when the babies come. Can you imagine?" She let out a bitter laugh. "They either robbed a bank or they're living in a dream world, a dream that can only come crashing down around them."

"I did hear that they opened escrow," Mary admitted.

Sharon looked suspiciously at Mary, then shook her head as if chalking it up to gossip. Of course, she was right to do so. "Those two don't have two pennies to rub together between them. If they pulled off something like this, it had to be by illegal means."

"It sounds like they want to help, and you can't fault them for that," Mary said gently.

"My boy's got a heart of gold, but he doesn't always show a lick of sense," Sharon said. "Do you have children?" She looked at Mary.

Mary nodded, thinking how her children had blessed her. "They all have a lot to learn."

"Don't we all," Millicent said with a light laugh and wave of the hand.

Mary and Sharon laughed with her.

"We really must get back to the shop," Mary said, standing.

Though as she and Millicent made their way back to the Impala, Mary's heart sank as she considered the desperate needs of the family. How could she blame Heidi if she somehow heard about the valuable book and found an opportunity to nab it with Cade as her accomplice, waiting outside the bookshop door that stormy night?

She and Millicent waved good-bye to Sharon and then climbed into the Impala.

They didn't speak until Mary pulled into the Grace Church parking lot. She had gone straight there on a bit of a mission.

She asked Millicent to wait in the car as she went to talk to Pastor Miles.

The pastor stood when he saw her at his office doorway, smiled, and extended his hand.

"Pastor Miles, I've just come from visiting a family who is in great need. I could tell they didn't have heat—the place was frigid." She gave him other details, including the family name and address. "I have the feeling they're in desperate need of food, warm clothing, and help with their utility bills."

As she wrote out a check to help the Gilbert family, Millicent appeared at her elbow, opened her wallet, and pulled out a few twenties.

"It's good to see people helping others. I don't have a church family of my own, but now that I'm alone, I think I'll start going again. My husband didn't like going to church, so when he died, we didn't have anyone we'd become close to. He was in business a distance away, and we had social contacts but no real friends."

Pastor Miles thanked Millicent, and after a brief chat with the pastor about church matters, Mary walked with the woman back to her car. As they walked, Mary reached for Millicent's hand. "No children?"

Millicent shook her head. "That's why Rebecca and her family are so important to me."

Mary opened the car door for Millicent, then moved to her own door, got in, and started the engine. When Millicent was buckled in, Mary spoke again. "Rebecca's family will always be there for you."

Millicent smiled. "I know, and I'm so grateful. It means so much that Rebecca opened her home to me at a time like this. I don't know what I would have done without her."

When they arrived at the bookshop, Mary helped Millicent out of the car and up the walk to the bookshop front door. As she opened it so Millicent could step through, she said, "Thank you for going with me."

"I was happy to," Millicent said. "There's something about Heidi that reminds me of myself at that age, though I never had children." She looked up at Mary, her eyes misting. "I was a little waif of a girl married to someone who was always getting into this business deal or that. I never knew what rabbit he might pull out of his hat next."

She laughed lightly and fluttered a hand. "But listen to me go on. I loved my husband, and he loved me. Oh, the good times we had. He took his work very seriously." Her eyes brightened with tears. "But he was romantic, seeming to know how to woo a girl even in the midst of some big business deal or whatnot. He brought me flowers—orchids were my favorites—and chocolate samplers, wrote little love notes and left them under my pillow." She reached for her handkerchief. "I loved him so much...and miss him. What will I do without him?"

Mary reached for the older woman's hand. As widows, they were sisters, and she understood.

FOURTEEN

◆◆◆

The wind huffed and puffed, keeping Mary from a sound sleep, and finally in the middle of the night, a loud gust rattled the windows so hard she sat up with a start. Her heart thudding, she reached for the light and then her glasses. At the foot of her bed, Gus was on full alert.

An errant branch banged the window again. She jumped again. Gus dove under the covers. The wind howled and moaned. She shivered. And waited. Listened.

She reached under the covers and rubbed Gus's head. He purred.

Mary fluffed her pillows, turned out the light, took off her glasses, and settled back. After all, it was only another storm blowing in.

Once her heart steadied, she smiled to herself. At least one could never call the weather dull in Ivy Bay. As the wind banged shutters and branches, she thought about the blessings the seasons brought to her little town, how new-fallen snow sparkled in the moonlight after a freeze, how dark winters gave way to early spring, and how May lilacs gave way to June roses and July sunflowers. How, during long summer evenings, she watched Betty work in her garden and then watched the bounty of vegetable gardens in the neighborhood as tomatoes ripened and corn grew tall, and then back to fall, when God painted Ivy Bay in vivid colors just for His people to enjoy. And the cranberries in her own backyard...oh, what a gift that fed the soul. The color. The joy of their scent bubbling on the stove with cinnamon and nutmeg at Thanksgiving.

As another gust of wind buffeted her window, her thoughts turned to the Gilberts, and she remembered how when she visited the previous morning Mrs. Gilbert had wrapped herself in a blanket to keep warm. She wondered how the family fared this night and wondered if she should have taken blankets and clothing and food rather than stopping by the church. But she also knew how proud people on the Cape could be, no matter their circumstances, and she hadn't wanted to do anything to cause Mrs. Gilbert embarrassment or distress.

Now, however, as she thought about them, she whispered a prayer for their well-being. And she prayed she'd done the right thing.

What would she do if Heidi and Cade were the thieves? What if they had taken the book out of great and desperate need? She had kept her emotions under wraps the day before, but now, her tears crept from the corners of her eyes and dripped onto the pillow. "Oh, Lord," she prayed, "You've said that when we help the poor, it's as if we're helping You, that even if we give a cup of water to a child, it is as if we're giving it to You. But, Father, sometimes the needs are too great. It takes more than just a few to make a difference."

She pondered the words of a great missionary who gave her life to serving the poor in India: "God does not call us to be successful; He calls us to be faithful."

"Lord, help me to be obedient and to do what I can...always. Give me eyes to see, really see, and not to look the other way. Ever."

She fell asleep again, though slept fitfully. After a few more tosses and turns, she switched on her bedside lamp again, swung her legs over the side of the bed, grabbed her glasses once more, and reached for her slippers with her toes. She slid into her robe, padded downstairs and into the kitchen, and put on some water for a cup of herbal tea. Gus followed along behind her.

It was three o'clock, too early to stay up, but by now, she was wide awake, and her mind was already hard at work puzzling the mystery of *The Murder of Roger Ackroyd*.

It had now been four days since the book disappeared, and she felt she'd made no progress. She'd talked to the mysterious Nigel Finnian and was pretty sure that he was married to none other than the so-called Laurie Block aka Leona Finnian. She'd called Orris Rathburn and now wondered if he was involved too—but she hadn't figured out how he played into the puzzle.

Even yesterday, after she dropped off Millicent at the bookshop, she'd stopped at the Chickadee Inn to talk with Laurie Block, but the woman had been nowhere around, and if proprietor Alexa Rose knew her whereabouts, she didn't say.

Mary carried her teacup into the living room, set it on the coffee table, and then sat down in a wing chair with a notepad and pen. She listed her primary suspect.

Number one was Nigel Finnian, collector of rare books.

Nigel had motive and opportunity. But a new thought occurred to Mary. If he had taken the book, why didn't he leave town immediately? But then it hit her: His wife was in town. His estranged wife. Mary strained to make the connection between their marriage and the book. Perhaps she left him because of money? The tabloids never seemed to get every detail right in stories like this, and perhaps that's something they'd left out. Had Nigel found out about the book and realized he could make some money off of it? On the other hand, if Nigel was a well-known rare-book collector, surely he had other valuable books in his possession that could make him some quick money. It didn't add up.

And then there was the confounding fact that Leona was wearing a disguise and had denied knowing Nigel when Mary had initially asked. Why? Did it have to do with the robbery after all?

Her focus shifted to Heidi and Cade, who had moved close to the top of the suspect list too—now that she knew about their house purchase. And of course, she couldn't forget about Bob Hiller, as much as she wanted to.

She jotted a note to check in with Lori Stone, the local Realtor, about home sales pending in Ivy Bay. At least it would be a starting point, and then she'd need to dig from there.

The clock was ticking. She needed to find the book. What if it was hidden right under her nose, ready to go up on auction or to be sold at any minute?

Little Isabella came to her mind, and she rose, notebook in hand, with new determination.

Still lost in thought, she headed to the kitchen to grind the beans and start the coffee. It had just finished brewing when Betty came in, dressed and ready to leave for another day of work at the Chickadee Inn.

Mary went over to the counter and poured another cup of tea. After the night she'd had, she needed a bit of a caffeine jolt to get through the morning. "Looking forward to our tea this afternoon, Bets."

"Me too. It'll be fun for you to see how far we've come decorwise in only a matter of days."

"Would you care for toast this morning?"

Betty nodded, and Mary dropped two slices of bread into the toaster as her sister got out the butter and jam.

They sat across from each other at the table, Mary said grace, and then asked, "And how are things between you and Alexa?"

"The past couple of days have been good. We see eye to eye on nearly everything. I suggested Cape Cod blue and gray with an accent of cranberry red for the primary color scheme. I found some wonderful plaids that pull the colors together. More traditional than country, yet sophisticated and warm at the same time. And, thank goodness, she likes antiques, which will fit in with the rest of the inn." She laughed lightly. "I'm pleased to say that she wants no ruffles or bows." She rolled her eyes. "Not that I was worried. But you never know."

"What about the book wars?"

"On hold for now. I'll do whatever she wants, although she certainly does have something against mysteries. One of our guests was carrying a Grisham, and I would have been able to see the judgmental smirk from a mile away."

"Well, to each her own, I suppose," Mary said.

"I suppose so," Betty said and exited through the garage door.

As soon as Mary arrived at the bookshop, she went to the computer to check the Internet for sales pending in Ivy Bay. She wanted to do a bit of homework before she called Lori. Several houses seemed to fit the bill for a large family. After studying the descriptions carefully, she narrowed the count to three, studied them online, going through the photos of the property, imagining a large family with in-laws and several children. One fit the bill perfectly. It called for nearly $30,000 as a down payment.

She immediately dialed Lori Stone at her real estate office. Lori answered on the first ring. They exchanged pleasantries, and then Mary asked about the house that she'd targeted as the likely one for a large family.

"I can't give you many details," Mary admitted. "But I need information about this house." She gave her the number listed online. "It's listed as 'sale pending' according to the ad. Can you tell me anything about it—without jeopardizing client confidentiality, of course?"

"Let's see," Lori said thoughtfully, and Mary could hear typing in the background. "I can tell you that the offer was close to the asking price, which delighted the seller. It's a short escrow, and the clients had the means to put down the asking amount. You already have the address, and if you're interested, you can drive out to see it." The typing stopped. "It's the old Joneses' house out near the pond. A real fixer but a rambling old place. And a steal at the price they're getting it for. It came on the market quite suddenly, and I knew my clients were looking for something, so I gave them a call...and well, we'll see. But it looks good."

Mary let out a pent-up breath. Opportunity and motive. She fought the disappointment, at the same time, understanding. "They've come up with the down payment?"

"Yes, but the funds don't have to be put in escrow for another, oh, say fifteen days or so. Loan approval pending too, of course."

Long enough to sell something valuable.

The morning went smoothly, customers coming in and out, carrying with them the smell of Sweet Susan's special of the week, red-velvet cake. Rebecca was coming in a little later this morning, but Mary was happy to handle the flow of customers herself.

After the initial morning rush slowed, Mary was hit with a near deluge of phone calls. She received calls from both Jack and Lizzie, who asked about the stolen book and how the investigation was coming along. Which reminded her to call Chief McArthur to see if he'd found out anything new. He said he hadn't, and she put down the phone in disappointment. She'd barely disconnected when Pastor Miles called to let her know that food and warm clothing had been taken to the Gilberts.

"They were so appreciative," he said. "Especially the young married couple..."

Then Henry called soon after.

"Any new developments?"

"No, nothing concrete."

"You sound like you could use some cheering up. How about if I come by and take you for a snack?"

Mary laughed. "That sounds wonderful."

"Breakfast rolls at the diner?"

"Perfect."

"How soon can you get away?"

Mary smiled into the phone. "How about as soon as Rebecca gets in, which should be any minute?"

"I'll be there."

———

Rebecca and Millicent arrived just after Mary ended the call with Henry. As usual, Millicent hobbled along with her cane, and this time, Rebecca carried her aunt's yarn bag, which seemed to be bulging with more than yarn. Rebecca placed it beside the rocking chair and then helped her aunt sit.

When she was settled, she reached into her tote and pulled out a Mozart CD, a small portable CD player, a Seaside Knitters Mystery paperback, and a skein of variegated yarn and a crochet hook and went to work. Mary exchanged looks with Rebecca when they moved to the front of the shop. Rebecca explained that Millicent had given more books and Mozart CDs—which she'd said helped enhance reading comprehension—to Heidi, and that she'd even been invited to dinner. She was becoming quite the surrogate grandmother.

Mary grinned. "How fun."

"And apparently, Aunt Millicent has even been teaching Heidi some basic crochet stitches to make things for the babies."

Soon after, as if on cue, Heidi arrived. Again, on the back of the motorcycle.

Laughing, she came into the shop and held up her hand, palm out. "Don't say it," she said. "I know I need to be careful."

Even Millicent raised her eyebrows, but she called Heidi to the back of the shop where the two began to carry on as if this had been their routine for years.

Two customers came in soon after, and Rebecca stepped over to help them find the novels they requested.

After a few minutes, Heidi helped Millicent set up the CD player, and Millicent asked Heidi to read to her. Soon the rhythm of her voice rose and fell with the background of Mozart.

It was a pleasant blending of voice and orchestra. Mary could almost hear Heidi pick up the rhythmic cadence of *The Magic Flute* as she read.

Mary was straightening and dusting the children's nook when Henry arrived. She looked up, met his eyes, and smiled.

"You look like you could use a break," he said as they stepped outside.

Mary drew in a deep breath and nodded. "I feel like I'm spinning my wheels. And getting nowhere fast." She bit her lip. "And the worst part about it is that time is passing too quickly. I think about Isabella, and this whole affair becomes much more than a mystery that needs solving. It's about a little girl's life, about the money her parents need to get her proper care."

They reached the diner, and Henry opened the door for her. Mary stepped inside.

They'd just been seated when Bob Hiller came through the door.

He spotted them and waved. Mary motioned him over. "How's Isabella doing?"

He shook his head slowly. "No change, but she's a brave little one. All smiles. Everyone at the hospital has fallen in love with her." He checked his watch. "I'm on duty and must be on my way." He searched Mary's face and then Henry's. "Thanks for asking. Everyone's doing what they can, praying, bringing meals to my son and daughter-in-law, just helping out in so many ways...but..." His voice broke off.

"It's the money, isn't it?" Mary finished.

He looked up a bit sharply, Mary thought.

"I mean, we know about the struggle with insurance, the move the doctors want to make to get her into Boston Children's Hospital."

He nodded, pressing his lips together so hard they were in a straight line and almost white. "Sometimes," he began, and then looked away. "Sometimes, situations like this can cause a man to rethink everything."

He lifted his hand and then, as if realizing his vulnerability, straightened up rather quickly. "I'd better go." He turned and headed for the door.

"Wait," Henry said and stood to go after Bob. Mary watched as Henry threw his arm about Bob's shoulders, and the two talked for a few minutes.

When Henry came back into the diner, he didn't speak for a moment. Then he said, "The man is desperate to help his children and granddaughter."

"Financially?"

He nodded.

"Apparently, the need is greater than they at first thought." He sighed.

"Oh dear," Mary breathed. "You don't think—"

Henry shook his head. "I hope not."

FIFTEEN

———◆◆◆———

M ary arrived at the Chickadee Inn for tea a few minutes early that afternoon with two of her favorite mysteries tucked in her handbag. A round table with a floor-length linen tablecloth was set for four in front of the tearoom fireplace, flames cheerily cracking and popping. A floral teapot sat at the table's center, with a matching teacup and small luncheon plate at each setting. Delicate silverware caught the glow of light streaming through windows on either side of the fireplace. At first, she thought the strong scent of cinnamon and nutmeg wafted from the kitchen, then realized tastefully decorated containers of potpourri had been placed at the entrance, the check-in desk, and in the parlor where she now stood. She sighed with contentment. Even if the scent wasn't from something baking in the oven, she still looked forward to the treats to come.

Through the window to the right of the fireplace, Mary could see a lone fishing boat on the bay, bobbing on the gentle waves. A flock of noisy gulls flapped and soared and flapped again above the boat, likely waiting for the fisherman to clean his catch and dump the leftovers back in the water.

Mary set her purse down beside the table, and just as she turned to admire the room and its cozy decor—even if it was too frilly for Alexa's "sophisticated" tastes—Alexa and Betty came down the stairs, their voices carrying.

A few minutes later, Laurie Block swept into the room in another gorgeous pants outfit and high-heeled fur-trimmed boots, and instantly, Mary knew she was looking at Nigel Finnian's wife. There was no doubt in her mind; the sparkle in the woman's eyes, though dimmed a bit it seemed, belied her true identity.

The woman's long red hair caught the light as she flipped it back with her hand. Smiling, she came over to greet the others. Mary tried to mask the urgency she felt to talk to the woman about Nigel. She had denied knowing him before, but now, Mary knew otherwise.

Alexa introduced Betty to "Laurie," and then invited Laurie to stay for tea. The woman accepted, and Mary was glad, but it did give her pause. When Mary had asked Laurie about Nigel when they'd first met, the woman obviously knew him, although she'd denied it. But if Nigel really had stolen from Mary, Laurie's denial suggested that she knew about the theft. Yet, if that was the case, why would Laurie be so willing to have tea with Mary and not want to run the other way?

"I'm glad you can stay, Laurie," Alexa said. "Please, everyone, have a seat."

After everyone took their places, they chatted about the beautiful antiques Alexa had used for the table settings.

"They belonged to my grandmother, and truly, they are priceless," Alexa beamed. "Now if you'll excuse me, I'm going to grab another table setting for Laurie, and I'll bring the cart of goodies from the kitchen. Be right back!" Alexa had the air of a woman quite proud of her wealth, and yet, she was unusually earnest in this setting.

While Alexa was gone, Mary had a chance to study Leona while she talked with Betty. The woman was colorful and animated. More than once, she tossed her hair—which Mary had to assume was a wig—or twisted it down the front of her shoulder, her fingers fluttering nervously.

She seemed to sense that Mary watched her, and turned, quizzically. Mary smiled and joined the conversation.

Alexa returned from the kitchen with a cart full of tea sandwiches, fruits, and pastries to the accompaniment of oohs and aahs.

The group fell into a pleasant conversation, Betty and Alexa soon enough explaining the details of the decor plan, with wide gestures and by finishing each other's sentences. Betty even pulled out a few swatches to share with the group, and Laurie was surprisingly engaged, as if she'd lost herself in the conversation.

Alexa began to tease Betty, then, bringing up the topic of the display books. "I keep telling her that our customers are the kind who expect only the highest literary quality, not paperback pulp."

"I, on the other hand," Betty said lightly, "think your clients will want to be entertained. And to me, mysteries are the height of entertainment."

Alexa's attention turned to Laurie. "Tell me, Laurie," she asked as she passed the plate of sandwiches, "what are your favorite nightstand books?"

Laurie took a cream cheese and watercress sandwich and passed the dish to Mary. "I admit I prefer light reading at bedtime. I love mysteries too. They can be humorous or serious, but I like something that keeps me turning pages to see what happened. A good old-fashioned whodunit."

"And we know about you and where you fall on the issue," Alexa said to Mary with a laugh.

"I confess," Mary said playfully, "you caught me. I love mysteries and actually find them to fall anywhere on the range of the literary scale—some very pulpy, you're right, but others, canonical. You're welcome to stop by my bookshop anytime. We'd love to see you." Mary said this to both Alexa and Laurie. "I sell lots of new editions of course, but also quite a few rare books."

"I'll have to take you up on that," Laurie said, reaching for another sandwich. "I'm looking for a rare book, actually—an Agatha Christie."

"Really?" Mary felt her eyes widen. "Which one?" This had to be a bit more than mere coincidence that she would ask about a rare Agatha Christie book.

"It doesn't really matter," she said and shrugged. "Though a first edition if possible. One of her earlier works."

Laurie smiled, and Mary noticed the dimple in her chin, her delicate bone structure. "I'm looking for such a book as a gift," she said. She stared at Mary, her gaze intense.

Mary nodded politely, but she was distracted. It struck her as strange that Laurie would bring up a rare Agatha Christie book at all. Or was it? In one of the articles Mary read online, the writer mentioned that Nigel Finnian was a collector of rare books. Maybe the woman was simply telling the truth. She was, after all, really Mrs. Nigel Finnian. Perhaps she just wanted to find a rare Christie book for her estranged husband.

Still puzzling the question but trying to keep the conversation going, Mary turned her gaze to Alexa and changed the subject back to the mystery genre. "Although, Alexa," she kept her tone light, "if you're not a huge fan of mystery, I suspect you might not be patronizing my shop anytime soon. So, I decided to bring a little of my shop to you." Alexa smiled graciously, and Mary pulled the two books out of her handbag. "I brought you two of my favorites by a terrific author named Ellis Peters."

"I've never heard of him." She raised an eyebrow but smiled. "But I'm willing to give him a try."

"They're British mysteries," Mary said, "and are set in the Middle Ages. The sleuth is a monk named Brother Cadfael. They take place in Shrewsbury, England, right on the Welsh border. They're quite popular."

"Thanks, Mary. That's really thoughtful of you. Although I think we both know that popular doesn't necessarily translate to good," she said. Then she sighed. "I hope I don't sound like a book snob. It's just that…well, years of prejudice are hard to overcome." She leaned forward. "Please, no hard feelings. I'll try. I honestly will. But tastes are tastes…"

Mary met her smile. "I'll be anxious to hear what you think."

Mary noticed that Laurie's gaze had drifted to the window, where in the distance, the bay shone in the sun and the gulls still cartwheeled above the lone fishing boat. Patches of ice sparkled here and there in the rocky sand.

Mary wondered if she knew she could see the little fishing cabin her husband was renting if she stood on tiptoe. Laurie turned back to the women, her gaze on Mary. For a moment, she didn't speak, then she said, "My favorite writer is new. Not yet published." She turned back to the window, obviously unwilling to say more.

If Mary had any doubt before that the woman in front of her was Leona Finnian in disguise, that last comment just proved it unequivocally. The love in her voice for the "new writer" matched the adoring expression of the woman in the newspaper photograph, looking at her husband: rare-book collector and aspiring writer. And possible thief.

So many questions remained, however. Again, why the disguise? Why was she in Ivy Bay if she was estranged from her husband who was also here? Why her interest in the same book that was stolen from the shop?

Did she hope for a reconciliation? Or was the disguise to keep from being recognized by media people who knew her from Boston society life? Maybe she was doing some sleuthing of her own, spying on her husband to see if he was being unfaithful?

As the tea came to an end, Mary asked Laurie if she could talk with her privately.

Laurie readily agreed, and after they stepped into the parlor on the far side of the entry, Mary said gingerly, "I recognized your photo from the *Boston Globe* society pages."

Laurie blinked. "I'm sorry...I don't know what you're talking about."

Mary didn't need Laurie to admit anything when the recognition in Laurie's eyes belied her denial. "Please let me try to explain," Mary said kindly. "I just wondered why the elaborate disguise."

Leona stared at Mary for a moment and then shook her head. "I can't say. Not now." She turned swiftly and practically ran to the stairs.

SIXTEEN

❖

The next morning, as soon as Mary put her feet in her slippers and slid her eyeglasses onto her nose, she walked to the window, pulled back the curtain, and gazed out. Snow fell in flakes the size of silver dollars and covered the ground rapidly. Its pristine beauty was breathtaking. It looked like the snowstorm was settling in to stay a good while.

She heard Betty stirring, so she slipped on her robe and headed downstairs. Her sister was standing by the window, peering out. She turned when she heard Mary approach.

"Good morning, Sis."

"Have you looked outside?"

"First thing I did when I got up." Mary walked over to stand beside her sister and looked out. Snowflakes the size of silver dollars were falling fast. "Looks like we're in for it today."

"I heard the snowplows earlier, but if we go out, we'll need to put on chains."

"We?" Mary quirked a brow.

Betty laughed. "Figuratively speaking. But we should call Kip Hastings before he gets busy with other jobs." They had reached the kitchen, and Betty glanced out the window. "From the looks of this, he may have quite a lineup of folks waiting for chains on their tires."

"See if he can move us to the front of the line." Mary ground the beans, started the coffeemaker, and reached into the cabinet for their mugs.

Betty dialed Kip. After a few minutes of conversation, she hung up. "It's a good thing we called early. He said he'd be over about nine."

They went into the living room and sat down with their coffee. Betty started a fire in the fireplace, and soon it was crackling and warming the room. Outside, the snow continued to fall.

Mary settled into the sofa facing the window and sipped her coffee. "Are you going to the inn today?"

"I left some fabric samples with Alexa yesterday, and we went through photos of furniture and accent pieces I'd pulled from magazines. She's going to think about it for a few days." She sat down in the chair next to Mary. "And it's just as well. If the snow keeps coming down at this rate, I really don't want to be out in it." She picked up her coffee mug. "How about you? Can you just close the shop today? I doubt that you'll have many customers on a day like today."

Mary grinned. "You never know. These Ivy Bay folks are a hardy bunch."

"No snow days for adults," Betty said, smiling.

Mary stood and walked to the window. The snow was coming down as thick and fast as before, and fog hugged the ground.

Betty came up and stood beside her. "I know you're hurting over the missing book."

"It's more than just puzzling over a mystery." She focused on the falling snow as she spoke. "I think about the needs all around us. After visiting the Gilberts, it brought it home to me. There are people whose needs are so great. I can't help coming back to the culprit being someone whose need overshadowed their sense of right and wrong." Bob Hiller came to mind as she spoke.

"Making wrong seem right to them," Betty added.

"Exactly."

She was still wondering if need could overshadow a person's sense of right and wrong as she settled onto the sofa. Betty sat beside her.

"Right versus wrong and deep, heartrending need brings us back to Isabella," Mary said, with a familiar ache in her heart as she added, this time out loud, "and Bob Hiller."

After a moment, Betty said, "Is Nigel Finnian still at the top of your list of suspects?"

Mary nodded. "And for a moment, I thought perhaps his wife was involved too. But now I'm not so sure." Mary had told Betty the night before what she'd discovered about Ms. Block also being Leona Finnian.

"Maybe talking about what you know for certain about each will help." Betty settled back and gave Mary an encouraging smile.

"Okay, here goes. Nigel and the woman we now know is his estranged wife are acting more than suspicious. At the same time, both are in town around the time of the book's disappearance." She quirked a brow. "Perhaps the other was meant to be."

"True," Betty said, "and Nigel was in the bookshop the night the book was taken."

Mary nodded. "And the following day, he stopped by the inn asking for Leona. He seemed upset that she was late to arrive. He'd been expecting her before the book chat."

"So maybe they were planning to work together to take it."

"But surely Leona would have never mentioned the book to me during our tea if she was responsible. And neither of them knew about the book chat…," Mary mused. "Although it's entirely possible that Nigel had heard about the book."

Betty leaned forward, her gaze intent as she followed Mary's reasoning.

"He couldn't have planned the power outage, though," Mary continued. "But then, no one could have. Still, Nigel is definitely at the top of my list."

"I agree. And who else?"

"Next would be Heidi Gilbert. She needed money for the down payment on the house they're buying. After seeing how they live, it's a real possibility."

"Plus, she not only had motive but opportunity," Betty added.

"True. More than once. During the blackout and when you and I were cleaning up and didn't know anyone else was in the shop. And she'd been in the shop before, so she knew about the back door and certainly could have tried to steal the book before the book chat but was then thrown off when I arrived early."

"Or maybe Nigel was in the shop when you arrived." Mary could tell that Betty didn't want to believe that Heidi was guilty. Mary didn't either.

Her mind raced. "You know, that's possible. If he did know about the book, he might have scoped out the shop before that evening and made up the part about just arriving. He could have even watched during the day, seeing where I put my purse, the key, the works."

"It fits," Betty said.

Mary sighed. "Remember, though, that the chief said there were no scratches or signs of break-in on either door. He would have had to have a key to the shop too."

"Or just been very good at breaking and entering."

Mary took a sip of coffee. "Okay. But nearly everything we've said about the Finnians could be true about Heidi and Cade Gilbert." She slumped back and watched the fire, shaking her head slowly.

"Who else?" Betty asked gently.

"I hate to say it, but we can't completely overlook Bob Hiller." She told Betty about hers and Henry's conversation with Bob the previous day. "But I just can't bring myself to ask him about it. It would be terrible to make an accusation such as that."

She got up and went over to the window, and Betty followed her. Without speaking, they watched the snow fall for a few minutes.

"But I do need to talk to him," Mary said. "I need to tell him about the gift of money that was to go to Isabella when the book sold. If he did steal the book, perhaps that information would draw a confession out of him."

First, though, she wanted to check on the Gilberts. Though she'd given a check to Pastor Miles and he'd said people from the church had seen to their needs, she wanted to see for herself that the electricity was turned back on. Sometimes, the power companies didn't get to such things as quickly as needed. Plus, as much as Mary didn't want to believe it, Heidi was clearly hiding something. Although she wasn't sure how, perhaps a visit to the Gilberts would bring her one step closer to finding out what.

———————

Kip attached the tire chains to the Impala, turned on the heater full blast, letting it warm as he backed it into the street, and turned the big car toward town. The snow still fell, and on the ground, it measured at least three or four inches.

"You be careful now," he said with a youthful smile as he opened the car door for Mary. "Can I do anything else for you? Do you need me to follow you to make sure you get to where you're going in one piece?"

Mary laughed, knowing he was teasing. "I'll be fine," she said as she handed him a bill with a tip for his work. She slid onto the seat behind the steering wheel, adjusted the window wipers and defroster. "I've been driving in snow since I was knee-high to a mosquito. But thank you for offering. I'll call if I get stuck."

He laughed. "Okay, then. Thanks." He trotted into the fog-laden, falling snow, his heavy red-plaid jacket and hat with ear flaps soon out of sight.

A few minutes later, Mary slowly turned on the road leading to the small manufactured house that belonged to the Gilberts.

She breathed a sigh of relief when, in the distance, she saw lights glowing through the windows. The power was on. As she drew closer, she could see that outdoors, the pristine snow hadn't been touched, which, in its beauty, masked the poverty and struggles of the family inside. Just as the lights in the windows cast a glow through the gray fog and rapidly falling snow.

She slowly rolled by, her chains crunching and clanking with each turn of the tires. She was abreast the house when she saw a figure in blue jeans emerge from the front door, look around a bit, stomp his feet, and grab a shovel. As the sound of the Impala carried toward him, though, he looked toward Mary. After staring in her direction for a moment, he walked toward the car.

"Ma'am?" he said as Mary rolled down the window. "Are you lost?"

She recognized the young man as Cade Gilbert. "No, I was just checking to see if everything was all right. When I came by last to talk to Heidi, I spoke with your mother. . . . " Mary faltered. She didn't want to cause any kind of embarrassment, but in most cases, it was best just to state the truth. "I was just worried about her, and I wanted to make sure your power was back on. Storms like this can take their toll, with power lines going down, that sort of thing."

"You came out to speak to my wife?" He leaned in closer so he could get a better look at Mary. "Oh, it's you," he said, smiling. "Mrs. Fisher from Mary's Mystery Bookshop."

"Yes, that's me."

"You've got quite a reputation around here."

"I do?"

He was grinning now. "You and Aunt Millicent are saints in Heidi's book."

"We are?"

"I've rarely seen Heidi so excited. Aunt Millicent gave her some Mozart CDs, and Heidi says they'll make us all smarter, and Rebecca from your shop loaned her the CD player. Now all we're hearing is like violins and stuff, on repeat." His grin widened, and Mary saw a clear sense of gratefulness in Cade's eyes. "And crocheting. Aunt Millicent taught her to crochet too. She's making me a stocking cap right now."

Mary felt her eyes watering. Cade's earnestness didn't at all match the roughneck troublemaker she'd expected him to be, and the growth that was happening in Heidi, regardless of whether she'd stolen the Christie book, was downright inspiring.

"Want to come in?" Cade offered. "It's awfully cold out here."

Mary looked at the illuminated house and shook her head. The Gilberts were doing just fine. "I really must be going. But I'm happy to see that your power is back on."

"Thanks, Mrs. Fisher. For everything," Cade said. "Take care."

He turned away, and she could hear him whistling something that sounded like *Eine kleine Nachtmusik*. "Cade…?" she called after him, intending to ask about the house he planned to buy for his family. And the item he had to sell for the down payment.

He turned and waved, not understanding she wanted him to come back to the car. "Thanks for everything," he called back to her.

She was almost glad for it. She couldn't bear to ask the question. She waved and rolled up her window.

How could this kind young man be a suspect? Her heart ached, knowing that it was possible.

———

Mary slowly made her way back to town, tire chains clanking rhythmically. She turned onto Main Street. The snowplow had been by earlier, and a high berm of scraped snow lined the street. If she parked in front of her shop, she would have to climb up and over the pile of snow to reach her front door. She smiled. Now that would be a sight, providing she could make it at all.

She continued to Jimmy's Hardware, which was clear, and pulled to the curb to park. She waved at the single customer who was just entering. The person, so bundled up she couldn't tell if she knew him or her or not, waved back. A few cars passed, their headlights shining through the falling snow.

Before she exited the car, she wound the wool scarf around her head and neck. She was greeted by the peaceful quiet of the new-fallen snow. There was nothing like that silence, and she looked up, tempted to catch a snowflake on her tongue the way she did as a child.

Her heart lighter than it had been that morning, she hummed a bit of *Eine kleine Nachtmusik* as she crunched through the snow to the entrance of Mary's Mystery Bookshop.

The minute she stepped inside the dark shop, she knew something was amiss. She froze in place, almost afraid to breathe. She hurried to the back of the store. The door was wide open. She heard the roar of a car engine on Meeting House Road and ran out the backyard gate to look. Tire tracks were embedded deep in the snow, but the vehicle that made them was long gone.

She knelt beside one of the tracks, and bending over, peered closely at the nubby-knobby detail.

The vehicle apparently had not needed tire chains.

SEVENTEEN

More curious than unsettled, Mary let herself back into the bookshop through the back door. She grabbed her cell phone and headed back outside to the side street. The snow was still coming down, though not as rapidly, but she wanted to get a photo or two of the tire prints, if possible. She zoomed in, made sure the flash was turned off, and took several shots from different angles. Then she tried a few with the flash. She hurried back into the shop, sat down at the computer, and plugged the phone into the computer to upload the photos.

Like magic, they appeared on her computer screen. Most looked washed out because they were white against white, but one seemed to give her the detail she was looking for. She examined it closely for wear, bald spots, or any unusual characteristics.

She Googled tire markings, and a list came up of the best-known brands in the United States. With a checklist of what to examine. There were no matches, so she tried foreign makes. Still nothing.

The vehicle didn't need chains to speedily get away when the driver heard Mary entering the front door. That took a skilled driver, someone used to driving in snowy conditions, and a vehicle with front-wheel drive and a quality engine. A BMW didn't fit the bill. Most were known for having rear-wheel drive. Though there were always those exceptions, she didn't know what they were called. There just might be a model specifically *made* for agility.

There was also the large, expensive SUV that had been parked in the Chickadee Inn lot the day she met Leona Finnian. The SUV could easily handle these road conditions. Bob Hiller drove an older car and likely would have had chains. And obviously, these were not the tracks of a motorcycle.

She huffed out a sigh and leaned back, lost in thought.

Then it hit her. Rumors had spread about the missing book. Could the word also have gotten around that she might have other valuable books tucked away?

Maybe this latest attempted break-in had nothing to do with the original. A coincidence?

Yet she still wasn't sure how whoever it was had access to the shop. Even if someone had taken her keys, they'd replaced them in her purse before the evening of the book chat was over.

It struck her suddenly that it couldn't have been Nigel. She'd had her keys with her to enter the shop that evening. In fact, by that logic, it couldn't have been Heidi or Bob either. She blew out a frustrated breath. Those three were her only suspects. But how could any of them have been guilty unless they'd had some other way of entering, or reentering, as the case might be? Mary supposed the person could have used a professional tool that would leave no mark, if there was such a thing. A tool that could be used in such a way by an amateur thief. Or maybe the thief wasn't an amateur.

She was getting a headache from thinking it through. She sat back with a sigh, thumping the eraser end of her pencil on the desk, puzzling all the ins and outs. Dead ends, all.

Trying to put aside her discouraging thoughts about the dead ends, she pulled a notepad from the top drawer. She scribbled some thoughts to follow up on later and then turned back to the computer. This time, she searched the archives of the *Boston Globe* for anything having to do with the marriage of Nigel and Leona Finnian. Almost instantly, a list appeared. Leona came from one of Boston's most prestigious families, so although she was marrying an unknown law student, everything about their courtship and marriage seemed to be fair game for the press.

Mary clicked the mouse on one link after another, scanning the photographs of their elaborate Christmas wedding in Boston. Finally, she came to word of the couple's honeymoon and where they'd gone. And a story of how they'd met—in a bookstore in Boston because of their mutual love of books.

She sat back and folded her arms. They honeymooned in Ivy Bay. Standing, she reached down to turn off the computer and flip off the desk light. After making sure the back door was locked—not that it'd seemed to matter—she started back through the shop toward the front door. The snowy day, it seemed, was keeping people at home. She couldn't blame them. Other shops along Main Street were nearly as empty of customers as hers. She was glad she'd given Rebecca the day off to spend with her family.

She quickly typed a note, printed it, and then taped it to the inside of the window, its message visible to anyone who might stop by: "Mary's Mystery Bookshop is closed due to snow today. If you're in need of a special book or have a question, please call and leave a message." She added the shop's telephone number.

She flipped the Open/Shut sign over to Shut and considered which clue she would investigate first. One thing was certain: She couldn't sit idly by and do nothing.

There were so many tricky pieces to this. For example, it made no sense to Mary why Leona would tell Mary about a rare Christie book if she'd taken part in the theft. In fact, it made no sense why Leona was willing to engage with Mary at all. Unless... was she trying to learn what other rare books Mary might have on hand? Was she planning on a repeat occurrence? Were those her tire tracks in the snow? Mary reached for the door handle again, pondering it all.

She stepped out into the chilly air. It was still snowing, though not at quite the rate as before. She walked to her car and got in, turned up the heater and defroster, and pulled out onto the street. She'd gone only a short distance, when headlights appeared behind her, approaching so fast, she had no time to get out of the way.

She closed her eyes, waiting for the impact... and praying.

There was no screeching of tires because of the snow, but she felt a slight bump in the rear of her car. And then saw the flash of headlights.

It took less than a minute for Nigel Finnian to exit his car.

He looked shaken. And yet also angry. "Mary! Are you all right?" he growled.

"I am. How about you?"

"Never better." His sarcasm was in full force.

Mary stared at the BMW. Its tires did *not* have chains, although she could have guessed based on the rear-ending. He brushed the snow from his head with a gloved hand. "I'm sorry, but if you're okay, I'm late for an appointment, and I must be going. Are you sure you aren't hurt?" He seemed more interested in his watch than in Mary.

He didn't wait for her answer.

He walked around to the rear of the car, then came back to the window. "No damage that I can see." His mouth was set in a harsh line, slightly curved downward at the corners. His demeanor gave Mary the chills.

With a shrug, he brushed the snow from his head again and walked to his car. He got in, clearly unconcerned with the traditional exchanging of information in an accident, revved his engine a few times, rocked the car forward and back, and then with a final revving, he shot out of the pile of snow. She pressed on her accelerator and had moved forward only a few feet when another set of headlights appeared in her rearview mirror. With a sigh, she decided to just let the person pass this time.

To her surprise, it seemed to be the same luxury SUV from the Chickadee Inn, heading the same direction as the BMW. However, the windows had such a dark tint she couldn't see the driver.

She turned the engine of the Impala, her tire chains crunching the snow almost in rhythm with her windshield wipers.

She followed the SUV just far enough behind to keep from being seen.

By the time Mary was within a stone's throw from the fisherman's shanty where the SUV had led her, the snow had stopped. In front of her, the SUV pulled up behind the BMW and stopped, and moments later a figure exited the car.

Mary parked down the street several car lengths away, then after wrapping her long scarf around her neck, she quietly stepped out of her car and closed the door.

It was now or never, Mary realized. Time to get some answers. Now that the two were together, it would be the perfect time to ask what they knew about the book. All secrets on the table, she prayed. It was time for them to tell the truth.

When she'd mentioned Isabella to Nigel, his heart had been touched. She'd seen it in his eyes. She hoped to see the same compassion in his wife's.

She trudged along, gingerly picking her steps. This close to the water, the icy air seemed to almost blow through her. She shivered and snuggled deeper into her goose-down coat. Though it was still morning, the storm clouds had settled so close to the ground, it felt like dusk. Strangely so.

Before she reached the cabin, she heard voices.

Though Nigel and Leona had entered through the back door, Mary didn't want to assume a visitor should do the same.

She moved slowly along the side of the house, through small snowdrifts that covered uneven sand. The wind stung her cheeks, and her glasses felt frozen to her nose. Her boots crunched along through the snow, and within a few seconds, the porch light flicked on, and someone peered through a window next to the door.

It was Leona Finnian, dressed much as she looked in the newspaper accounts. Inches shorter, brown hair, and wearing the cameo at her neck. She hurried past her husband down the stairs and answered the door.

"Mary Fisher, uh. Is something wrong? I suppose we forgot to exchange insurance information after our little bump there." Nigel was clearly trying to stay nonchalant. "And I suppose I should introduce you. This is my . . . wife, Leona. Leona, this is the proprietor of a nice little bookshop in town."

"We've met," Mary said, locking eyes with Leona who nodded, looking unsurprisingly nervous.

"Oh. Well, good. Is there something you need, Mrs. Fisher?" Nigel said.

"I told you when we last talked, Nigel, that something very valuable was taken from my shop. And I fear you know what it is."

Nigel rolled his eyes. "Not this again. Look, Mrs. Fisher, we don't have time to talk right now," Nigel said, letting out a weary sigh. "Please, leave us alone."

Leona offered nothing but silence and a sympathetic look. Nigel closed the door, leaving Mary standing in the snow.

Mary stood there for several minutes, then, taking a deep breath and whispering a quick prayer, she knocked on the door.

After a moment, Leona answered. "Mary, I'm sorry. But you really have caught us at a bad time."

Leona and Nigel were either really good actors or genuinely had no idea what Mary was talking about. She would try the Isabella route again. "There's a child," she said pleadingly, "who needs our help. Without it, she may not get the kidney transplant she desperately needs. And if you can help her, you must tell me the truth about why you're in Ivy Bay."

Nigel moved forward and stared at Mary, and then turned to his wife. "This is ridiculous. It's a ploy to get us to admit to something we didn't do. Don't listen. Don't fall for it."

He'd never looked more guilty than at that moment. Mary wondered briefly if she should barrel in and demand to search the premises. She could almost feel the weight of the book in her hands.

"Please hear me out," she said. But the door had already begun to shut.

EIGHTEEN

◆◆◆

Mary sat in her car, letting the engine warm for a few minutes. She'd just released the emergency brake and turned on the lights when Leona appeared beside her window.

"The child," Leona said when Mary rolled down the window. "Please tell me more."

Mary could see by her red-rimmed eyes that she had been crying. "Nigel won't tell me what all this is about. I don't know what to think."

Mary decided she would lay the cards on the table. If Leona was guilty, she seemed ready to confess. If not, it was not as if the valuable book was much of a secret anymore. So she told Leona about the disappearance of the book and how the proceeds would have gone to Isabella Hiller, a critically ill child, and her parents. She also mentioned that Nigel had been in her shop the night the book disappeared.

Mary could barely make out her features in the dim glow of the dashboard lights, but she could see that Leona looked shocked. "You're here because you think my husband stole your book?" She blinked and bit her lip. "That's why he's so angry with you." Then she studied Mary.

Mary sighed. "I haven't mentioned the book specifically, for many reasons, but yes. Although I'm not sure I'm the only one he's angry with. He seems angry at the whole world right now."

Leona looked down at the snow, kicked a bit off her shoe, then looked back up at Mary. "Everything is falling down around him, his career, his standing in the community, our marriage...." She shrugged. "You name it."

"I understand," Mary said gently. She'd read every detail she could find in the online accounts. Their recent separation, Leona's accusations of infidelity, the charges against Nigel for misconduct—and the resulting tarring of his less-than-stellar career. Leona didn't have to tell her anything. Mary had read it all.

The only thing she hadn't known was if the couple had used the stories as a cover for coming after the book. Stealing the book for Nigel's collection. He had been called ruthless by colleagues, by both enemies and friends. In Mary's book, ruthless wasn't too far from dishonest, which wasn't too far from thievery.

She looked up at the woman standing beside the car. Again, Mary wondered if she was a good actress. Or maybe she really was as sad as she now seemed.

Leona had begun to cry quietly. "I don't know whether to be angry, sad, or both." She looked at Mary hesitantly, as if unsure whether to open up.

Mary gave her a warm and encouraging look, knowing that no matter what this woman may have done, she deserved tenderness.

Leona continued. "Should I throw in the towel or try to make things work? I only know we can't go on like this. He invited me here tonight to talk things through. Then he starts in like the trial attorney he is, making accusations about my behavior. He accused me of trying to spy on him by using a disguise."

That had been one of Mary's theories too. "Weren't you?"

She sniffed. "Well, yes. I was. There've been rumors at our country club…about another woman. I figured out where he'd come. This little shanty belonged to his grandfather. We honeymooned here." Mary nodded, but Leona didn't seem to notice that Mary wasn't surprised by this information. Which was just as well. It was too soon to reveal that she had done her research on both the Finnians online.

"I've never been one to carry off anything deceitful," Leona said, smiling through a few lingering tears.

Mary wanted to believe her, but there was one more way to prove that Leona was innocent. She would invite Leona to her shop. A return to the scene of the crime.

"Tea and sympathy does wonders for the soul," Mary said, clapping her hands decisively. "And I'm a good listener. Why don't you follow me back to the shop? We can talk. I was married for many years before my husband passed. We had some rough spots, believe me. All couples do, but it's worth trying to work things out."

Leona nodded. "I'd like that."

On the way back into town, the big SUV loomed behind Mary the entire way. Again, she parked just outside the hardware store because of the snowplow piles left in front of the bookshop. Leona parked the SUV behind her, and they waded through wet snow to the bookshop entrance.

Mary started the fire and got things ready for tea, then sat opposite Leona in one of the two chairs in front of the hearth.

Leona's eyes were still red-rimmed and swollen. She pulled out a tissue and, dabbing her nose, looked around the shop.

"You have a delightful little place here," she said, and stood to have a closer look at a nearby bookshelf. She ran her fingertips across book spines, almost lovingly. "Beautiful, truly beautiful," she said, stopping to read a few titles. "What a wonderful collection."

Then she headed to Betty's teapot collection in the front window. "And this display...who designed the layout?"

"Betty. She changes the display pretty frequently. I'm lucky to have her."

"It's adorable." She picked up the same whimsical teapot, a Mary Engelbreit, that Millicent had admired.

As she moved it, the rattle of something metal clinked against the ceramic finish.

She frowned. "Do you keep something in here?"

Mary reached for the teapot. It definitely rattled as it moved. Coins perhaps? Of all things...

She frowned and lifted the lid. "Well, this certainly is a surprise." She peeked in. A small key ring with a single key lay inside.

She looked up at Leona who shrugged, seemingly uninterested, and wandered to a bookcase to browse.

Mary reached for the key and held it in her palm, staring. Then she held it to the light. It was newly cut. A copy of the original!

Her head spun with new possibilities...and narrowed the field of suspects considerably.

The teakettle sounded and, dropping the key in her pocket, she then placed the Engelbreit teapot back in the window and went to fetch their tea things. When she returned a few minutes later, Leona was standing by the shelf of Agatha Christie novels.

"I didn't say much when you were defending the genre to Alexa Rose the other day, but Nigel and I both love mysteries." She turned from the shelf and smiled. "Though, of course, there are plenty of fine writers we like in other genres." She walked back over to where Mary had set the tea tray on a table between the two chairs.

"Once Nigel and I get to talking about books, there's no stopping us." Her eyes misted. "We can talk about books and stories and mysteries until the wee hours of the morning. At least we used to."

"Your husband collects first editions, I understand," Mary said.

Leona gave Mary a sharp look but then quickly softened. "Yes. Yes, he does." She swallowed hard. "He's always on the lookout for something extremely rare, something that no one else has or could possibly get." She stared into the flames. "He's very competitive that way."

Mary considered her words. Perhaps two things were going on here: a broken marriage, a high-powered attorney who'd gotten his priorities in such a mess that he stooped to thievery, and a heartbroken wife who followed him to the place of their honeymoon, hoping to patch things up.

One thing didn't add up: He had known she was coming and had stopped by the Chickadee Inn to see why she was late. Mary had heard his words to Alexa about her guest, the guest Mary now knew was his wife.

But did any of this remove them from her list of suspects? She knew for certain they were husband and wife, and if she could believe Leona, they were in the midst of a troubled marriage. That seemed real. But there was still a niggling in the back of her mind making her wonder if they might have planned the robbery and used their split to get them out of the Boston social spotlight. Then they'd be free to steal the book in this little town, hide out in plain sight, and when the hoopla died down, return to Boston to get on with their lives.

She leaned forward. "I heard your husband ask Alexa about you the day after the book went missing. He wanted to know why you were late. He mentioned the death of something. What do you think he meant?"

"Death of our marriage, perhaps. He can be rather melodramatic," she said. A pink hue tinged her cheeks, and she let her gaze drift away from Mary. "Though when we talked earlier, he seemed not to care one way or the other."

"Maybe that's just his pride talking."

Leona nodded and then a tiny smile curved the corners of her mouth upward. "That he's got in abundance."

"How did he know when to expect you?"

"I'd written the hotel name and phone number on a page in my planner, and apparently he spotted it. He knew where

I planned to stay, and my arrival date." She cast her eyes downward for a moment. "Like I said, I'm not very good at deceptions. And when Alexa told me that he had been looking for me, it gave me hope that he still cares."

Calendar page? Mary sat back, remembering the torn piece of paper she'd found on the floor the night of the theft.

"But you were delayed because of the bridges being out."

"Exactly." She took another sip of tea.

Mary's mind was racing. The piece of torn paper was a clue as to who had been where when the lights went out the night of the theft. That put Nigel in the middle of the action. Suddenly, she needed to know that neither of them planned to leave town. She forced herself to sit back, relaxed and smiling. "Do you still think you might work things out? You said the other day that you planned to stay indefinitely. Have you changed your mind?" She leaned forward and sipped her tea.

Leona looked stricken. "I'm inclined to just leave for home tomorrow. He clearly doesn't want me here." Tears filled her eyes again.

"Don't give up yet. My advice, albeit unsolicited," Mary said, giving a rueful smile, "is to stay, no matter what. Offer your husband forgiveness, mercy, and unconditional love." She spoke gently, remembering her husband, remembering his love. Their love. A love that was worth fighting for. No matter what Leona and Nigel were going through, no matter if Leona had spoken the whole truth or not about their marriage, Mary's words came from the bottom of her heart.

Mary poured more tea into each cup, took a sip of hers, and then leaned forward. "I hope you'll work on things. It's important, believe me."

Leona stood abruptly. "I really must be going."

Mary stood with her.

"Thank you. For the tea and comfort. You provided a good listening ear."

Mary walked her to the door. As Leona put on her coat and wrapped a fringed scarf around her neck, Mary said, "Your husband isn't missing an antique comb, is he? Perhaps something that's been in the family for a century or so?" She'd already asked Nigel but wondered if she might get a different answer from his wife. She would leave no stone unturned.

Leona tilted her head and frowned. "Not that I know of, but he does have a tendency to pick things up at antique shops, flea markets, and the like, that I don't know about at the time." She laughed lightly. "I used to call him 'sticky fingers.'" Realizing what she'd said, she turned red.

Mary patted her arm. "That's all right. I knew what you meant."

As Leona pulled out into the street, Mary stood with her back against the door and let out a long sigh. She patted her pocket where the key was tucked away and thought of the planner page that had given away Leona's whereabouts.

With another long sigh, she closed the shop. It had been a long morning and not because of customers visiting her shop. Not a single person had called since she left her note. It seemed that the bone-chilling snow day had kept at home those who usually frequented her shop on a Saturday morning.

The empty street struck her as eerie as she got into the Impala and started the engine. She shivered again as she pulled into the street and headed home for lunch.

NINETEEN

———◆◆◆———

After lunch with Betty, Mary headed to the hospital. The sky was clearing with patches of sunlight now showing between the clouds. The snow that had fallen that morning sparkled in the sunlight. The air was frosty enough to see her breath and steam her glasses as soon as she stepped inside.

She went up to the reception desk and asked if Isabella Hiller was still in the same room. In previous visits, the room numbers had changed, depending on the treatment Isabella was receiving. The volunteer, a pleasant woman Mary didn't recognize, smiled and checked her computer.

"Yes, she's in the same room. You may go up to the third floor," she said, "to the waiting area. Only two people are allowed in at a time, and you'll have to gown up."

Mary had visited Isabella and her parents before, and she knew the term. Isabella was in a very delicate state right now because of her treatment and was highly susceptible to germs. Gowning-up meant putting the gown on over her clothing, wearing a mask and gloves and covers on her shoes.

She smiled her thanks and made her way to the elevator.

When she arrived in the large, airy waiting area, Bob Hiller sat near some double swinging doors, leading to the nurses' station. Bob looked up, smiled, and then stood as Mary approached.

"Thank you for stopping by," Bob said. "Isabella loves having you come. Amanda and Gabriel are with her right now, and she's in good spirits. It's hard to see her in that hospital bed, but we're hopeful that things will go smoothly once we can get her to Boston Children's."

His voice and body language said he couldn't wait another minute to see his granddaughter. "Do you want to come in with me?" He hesitated near the double swinging doors that led to the nurses' station.

Mary hesitated. "Bob?" she said. "Could we talk first? Just for a minute." He turned and looked at her.

She took a few steps closer. "There's something I need to tell you."

"What is it?" His brow furrowed. "Are you all right?"

"Yes, yes. I'm fine. . . . You know about the rare book— *The Murder of Roger Ackroyd*. Well, it was taken from my shop last Monday night."

His eyes widened. "Oh no. That's terrible!"

"I know. It's especially terrible because I had just arranged to sell it to a dealer for $31,000, and the dealer had arranged for a courier to pick it up the next morning."

"Oh my. That's a lot of cash," he said. "I'm so sorry for your loss. Are there any clues as to who could have taken it?" His eyes were clear and honest. His concern for her, real. But was there something else?

"What I wanted to tell you was that all the money was going to go to Isabella for whatever needs weren't paid for by insurance." Bob's expression froze for a minute, and then his body sank in a deep sigh.

"That would have made such a difference. A huge difference."

"I would have told you earlier, about the gift I mean, but didn't want you to know how close we came"—Mary hesitated—"only to have it snatched away."

For a moment, Bob remained silent. Then he turned back. "It means a lot even so. Just the thought that you would do this for her, for our family, means a lot."

"I haven't given up hope," Mary said. "I don't want you or Amanda and Gabriel to either." She touched his arm, and her plan to reenact the original book chat came to mind. If she hinted to Bob that he would have an opportunity to bring the book back—if he was indeed the one who'd taken it—and he could do so without being caught...perhaps he'd take the bait. She'd told Heidi and Nigel about the stolen book too, for the same reason. "In the meantime," she said, keeping her tone casual, "I'll look forward to seeing you at the book chat on Monday. Hopefully, everyone who was there last week will show up again. I've come to believe that the guilty party is someone who was at our first chat. Who knows, maybe the thief will realize the error of his or her ways and bring the book back."

Bob's head flew up and he looked at Mary with a hint of urgency. "Please, why don't you go ahead and visit with Isabella for a time? Gabriel and Amanda are with her right now, and they'll love to see you. I need to make a phone call."

Wasn't Bob, just moments ago, itching to visit Isabella? Why, now, did he suddenly have to make a phone call?

Mary nodded, turned, pushing through the double doors, and then walked down to Isabella's room. Isabella's parents were standing just outside their daughter's room. They gave Mary the latest medical update as she donned her gown, mask, gloves, and elasticized shoe covers.

"If we can get the go-ahead, they can begin the preparation for the transplant," Amanda, Isabella's mother, said. "But there are still some glitches because of the insurance issues...."

Gabriel came up and put his arm around his wife. "We're so thankful for the prayers and support from everyone at church, from all our friends." He smiled. "The books you've brought by bring her such joy."

Amanda gave her a hug. "Thank you."

As soon as Amanda had tied the back of her gown, Mary reached for the doorknob.

The first thing she noticed was the glowing smile Isabella gave her as she stepped through the door. She sat up in her bed, pillows fluffed behind her, dressed like a little princess in a pink flannel nightie with ruffles around her neck and a matching knitted pink cap with knitted flowers around the brim. She looked like she was hosting a party.

"I love Saturdays," she said, her thin fingers laced together above her tummy. "Nurse Beth says I have more visitors than anybody else in the whole hospital. Ashley and her mommy were here a bit ago. Ashley brought me pictures from my friends at school."

Mary drew up a chair so she could sit near the bed. "I'm glad you liked the Junie B. Jones books. Which one was your favorite?"

Isabella grinned. *"Aloha-ha-ha!"* Her eyes lit up. "I'm already ready for more. Do you have any?"

"I do." She handed Isabella a bag with three more books tucked inside. "How about these three? *Judy Moody, M.D.: The Doctor Is In!*, *Judy Moody Gets Famous!*, and *Judy Moody Saves the World!*"

"Yay!" She clapped her hands. "I love Judy Moody mysteries. Ashley brought me some Fancy Nancy books too. I want to be an artist and draw pictures like that someday." She sighed happily. "I love to draw."

Mary thought it amazing that whenever she stopped by to see this little girl, her own spirits were lifted. Isabella had a contagious optimism, despite her extreme fatigue, a symptom of her disease. Depression was also a symptom, but if the child experienced it, her naturally bubbly spirit hid it from view. Mary suspected the little girl had moments of fear and doubt, but when she had visitors, she always managed to give each one the gift of a smile.

"Daddy said I might have to move to another hospital. But I like this one. I can see the ocean from here." She pointed to the window. "I can even see fishing boats. Last summer, I saw lots and lots of boats, sailboats and speedboats, and people water-skiing. And seagulls too. And yesterday I saw snow falling. Great big flakes that seemed like they were floating."

She was quiet for a minute. "And I like Nurse Beth and Nurse Amy and Nurse Melinda and all the nurses here. They say I'm their favorite because I'm so happy all the time. But I think they tell all the littlest children that." She shrugged, played with her fingers, and looked up at the IV. "It doesn't hurt," she said. "But I'll be glad when I don't have it stuck in me anymore."

They talked for a few more minutes, and by the time the visit was over, Mary found herself laughing and smiling more than she had in days. She couldn't believe it hadn't even been a week since the book was stolen from her shop. Knowing the sale of the book could help this sweet girl so much, every moment the book had been gone felt drawn out.

When Mary stood, she wanted to hug and kiss the little girl, but transplant patients were vulnerable to germs, and the slightest touch could jeopardize the treatment.

Mary blew her a kiss, and the little girl, used to the drill, giggled as she reached out, caught it, and brought it to her lips with a loud smack. No wonder this child had more visitors than anyone else in the hospital.

When Mary reached the outer lobby, Gabriel and Amanda were sitting in an area off to one side with Pastor Miles, who was praying with them.

Bob Hiller was nowhere in sight.

———

Mary was still thinking about Isabella and her grandfather when she pulled up in front of the bookshop a few minutes before two o'clock. Betty pulled up behind her, tire chains rattling, set the brake, and then got out of the car with a bit more speed than usual. Up and down the street, now that the sun was peeking out, more shoppers had ventured out.

As Betty made her way toward Mary, her eyes were bright with merriment, and judging from her expression, laughter looked ready to spill from her lips.

Mary tilted her head. "You look ready to explode with laughter."

"I am. I am. And I can't wait to tell you. But let's go inside first. It's too cold to stand out here for my tale."

Mary unlocked the shop and stood back so Betty could enter. She would return home for Gus later; it had been too cold to leave him in the car during her hospital visit. She hadn't asked Betty to bring him because she'd planned to stop by the inn. She missed his furry presence.

Mary turned on the heat and ignited the gas fireplace while Betty put on water for tea. After the gloom of the early morning, Mary especially enjoyed Betty's cheerful presence. That thought reminded her to check messages.

She walked over to the phone. No one had called.

Finally, they sat down in front of the fireplace, Betty in their grandmother's rocker and Mary in the overstuffed chair beside it. She grinned at her sister. "Okay, tell me ... "

Betty leaned forward. "You will not believe what I found this morning."

"At the inn?"

She nodded. "You will absolutely not believe it!"

Mary seldom saw her sister filled with such obvious glee. She couldn't help laughing. "What? The suspense is killing me."

"Well, I was looking through some cabinets in the office area of the inn for some interior-decorating magazines and swatches I'd loaned Alexa the other day, when to my amazement...in a dark corner, away from the line of sight, did appear..." Her eyebrows shot up.

"What?" Mary laughed. "Please, tell me."

Betty leaned forward conspiratorially. "Paperback books."

Mary waited, as Betty's eyes twinkled and her face became even more animated.

"Paperback books of *all* kinds."

"You're kidding!"

"But they're different than you might expect. Strange and old. Very old."

"As in, how old?" Mary asked, turning over the new information in her mind.

Betty turned back to look at Mary. "Judging from the artwork on front, more like drawings really, I would say maybe eighteen hundreds. And they look like originals of whatever they are. Not copies. Yellowed with age. Brittle pages. I've never seen anything like them."

Mary had seen such books, usually in antique shops. "Could they be dime novels?"

Betty frowned. "Those old Westerns written in the nineteenth century?" She fell silent for a moment and then tilted her head, her eyes brightening. "You're amazing. I never thought of that."

"They were more than just Westerns. They were mysteries, adventure stories, and yes, Westerns. Very popular." She paused, thinking about Alexa's collection. "She must not care much about them if they're not out on display. She obviously cares about antiques. These books fit into that category.

"But they don't fit into her decor," Betty said with a laugh. "And they're definitely pulp fiction."

"I'd love to see one," Mary said. "What a treasure. I wonder where she found them."

"There's quite a stack. I would say maybe two dozen or more."

"Did you ask her about them?"

Betty shook her head. "I thought she'd see me as invading her privacy, even though I'd been getting magazines and swatches out of the same cupboard in her presence during the last few days."

"She wasn't there, then, when you found the books?"

"No. Even so, I didn't feel I should thumb through something that I wasn't meant to see."

"Would you mind if I asked her to see them?"

"No, not at all. I had a legitimate reason to look in that cupboard. I don't think she would think of me as a snoop."

She grinned at Betty. "Do you want to go with me?"

"Right now?"

"No time like the present." She glanced at her watch. "We've got nearly an hour before the shop opens. Is Alexa at the bed-and-breakfast?"

"Probably just finishing serving breakfast."

"Perfect," Mary said, grabbing her purse.

A few minutes later, she pulled up in front of Chickadee Inn. Betty got out of the Impala on the passenger side as Mary slid from behind the steering wheel.

Alexa greeted them with a smile as they entered and asked them to wait while she finished a guest's checkout.

"I found a stack of interesting books, antiques, I think, in one of your cupboards," Betty said. "I was just telling my sister about them...."

Mary smiled at Alexa as she broke in excitedly, "From the description, it sounds like you have some dime novels on your hands."

Alexa raised her eyebrows, not looking entirely pleased.

"They're valuable," Mary said. "Extremely."

"But pulp fiction, nonetheless." Alexa sniffed.

"I'd love to see them."

Alexa hesitated, then finally led them down a hallway to a supply cabinet. She pulled out the stack and set them on a table.

Mary touched the top one gently. "I've heard about these for years, but I've never seen one in person."

Just then, the bell at the front desk jingled. "Please excuse me," Alexa said, "I think a guest needs me, but feel free to look through the books. They're valuable to me, but not for reasons you might think."

Mary and Betty exchanged puzzled glances. Mary gently thumbed through a few, noting the handwritten name scrawled across the title page with a date. Each name was the same and written in a childish hand. But the dates changed with each book, starting with the earliest: 1860. Toward the bottom of the stack, she pulled out the most recent, dated 1907. The childish handwriting changed with the dates, in the latter years, obviously written in an adult hand.

"These are amazing," she breathed. "I wonder if Alexa knows the treasure she has here. Look at these titles: *The Privateer's Cruise and the Bride of Pomfret Hall, The Forest Spy: A Tale of the War of 1812,* and *The King of the Wild West's Cattle War.*"

There was something about just holding these well-read and well-loved books that warmed her heart. She noticed a piece of paper had been inserted into one of the books, obvious only because it looked modern and brighter than the pages of so long ago.

Betty was just as engrossed as Mary was but looked up when Mary drew out the sheet of paper.

"Look at this," she said. "It's a list, beginning with the name that's inscribed on the books: Greenfield Hill, age twelve in 1860, then it goes on to list his wife Beatrice and then their descendants and their spouses, ending with Alexa Rose, unmarried and the current date."

Mary swallowed hard. "No wonder Alexa loves antiques. These are incredible." She looked down at the list, then turned it over. A hastily written Web site was scrawled on the back. "Talk about a jarring ride back to the present." She laughed.

Betty gave her a quizzical look. "Jarring to be ripped back to the present after spending time in the nineteenth century. You can picture this twelve-year-old reading by the light of a fireplace, then imagine a twelve-year-old reading his favorite book online." She laughed, shaking her head.

Long after they said their good-byes to Alexa, Mary pondered the dime novels and the names on the list. They didn't mean anything to her right now in connection to the book she desperately needed to find, but something told her it might be important later.

Betty raved about the find all the way back to the shop and was still talking about it when they exited the car.

Mary couldn't wait to get to the computer to do more research on dime novels.

But as soon as she opened the shop, it filled with customers, and she didn't have time to spend a single minute at the computer.

Even so, something about the list nagged at her mind. And about the way Alexa avoided her gaze when she and Betty thanked her and left just a few minutes before.

She looked as if she were keeping something from them. What was it, and why?

TWENTY

N igel and Leona arrived in their large SUV just as Betty pulled out of her parking space behind Mary's.

From inside her shop, Mary studied their faces in confusion as Nigel opened the door and stood back to let his wife pass. He'd shaved and wore more presentable clothes—jeans, black turtleneck, denim jacket, and a tweed windsor cap. Leona, also in jeans and a denim jacket, studied him without expression as he reached for Mary's hand and shook it.

"It's a surprise to see you two here." Mary studied Nigel, wondering if he was avoiding looking at the bookcase on purpose.

"Actually," Nigel began, his face rather soft compared to how it had looked earlier, "we want to thank you for what you've done for us. Leona told me about your conversation this morning, your straight talk about marriage. We've made a commitment to hold on to what we have."

Mary was thrilled to hear it, although surprised to hear it coming from Nigel. And so soon, which caused her to be more than a little suspicious. Could she trust anything he might say right now? There was still something harsh in his expression, a distance that Mary had noticed the first night she met him. It troubled her to think that though he was saying all the right words, this might be an act. He may be sincere about wanting to rekindle his relationship with his wife, but that didn't mean he hadn't taken the book. And then there was the issue about the key. Did that take him off the hook? Should she remove him from the list of suspects?

Perhaps she should. But there was something in him that kept her from letting him go completely. She suddenly wished she'd had time to call Rebecca about the key, but she hadn't had a spare minute.

Mary gestured to the chairs by the fireplace. "Would you like some coffee or tea?" When they nodded, they all moved to the refreshment table.

"I should be angry," Nigel said as they began to pick from Mary's selection of tea. "You've all but accused me of a serious crime because of your missing book." He surprised her by looking sheepish. "I suspect that my reputation in Boston might have led you to that conclusion."

Mary smiled gently, surprised that Nigel was bringing up the topic this time. "Well, that and opportunity. You were here the night it was taken."

"What about motive?" he said, obviously playing the lawyer.

"You're a collector of rare books; you told me you were especially fond of Agatha Christie; *and* your wife told me that you were looking for an early edition of an Agatha Christie book."

Surprise registered on Nigel's face. "A *Christie* book? That's what you're missing?"

"Yes. *The Murder of Roger Ackroyd*."

"Well, I'll be. You're right; I have been in search of that book. But I didn't know you had it." He glanced at his wife, then back to Mary. "You don't still think I'm guilty, do you?"

She didn't know. Not really. In truth, no one had been crossed off her list. Alexa included, who seemed to be hiding something. Mary still suspected Heidi too, and she couldn't cross Bob Hiller yet off her list, much as she wanted to.

"The jury's still out," she said playfully. "But if you want to find out the answer, come to our second Winter Warmth Book Chat tonight. Leona, we'd love to have you too." She had thought earlier about re-creating the scene of the crime, so to speak, and that had become her plan. If she could once again gather all the same people who were in the shop the night the book was stolen, and if she could coordinate events just so, she may be able to pinpoint the culprit.

The two exchanged glances, then looked back to Mary. "We'll be here," Nigel said.

Mary stood as the couple exited the shop, suddenly feeling the fatigue of a very long day. And it wasn't even noon. She also had a sweet tooth. Perhaps this afternoon would be a good time to take Ashley up on her request to make cookies together. It'd be fun and relaxing, exactly what she needed.

She pulled out her phone and called Rebecca, who answered on the fourth ring. It was Rebecca's day off, but she knew her friend wouldn't mind a phone call from Mary, anyway.

"Hi, Rebecca. I'm wondering if this afternoon would be a good time to pick up Ashley and do some cookie baking. I found a new recipe she'll love—melted snowmen, made with marshmallows."

"She'd love that," Rebecca said. "Would you like for me to watch the shop?"

"We're not overcome with customers. I was planning to close early, but if you'd like to come in, that would be even better."

"Aunt Millicent said something about helping Heidi with her reading again. Maybe they'd like to come in with me."

"That would be great."

"We're all pretty sad around here," Rebecca added. "Aunt Millicent said that she needs to be on her way. She has a convention she's been invited to, and now, she's feeling strong enough to get out on her own."

"We'll miss her," Mary said. "I've enjoyed the time she's spent in the shop."

"I hope the weather is good for her travels. I hate the idea of her on the road, especially a long trip in the winter—and at her age. We cut it close last Monday, but still. Thankfully, her four-wheel drive has good tires. But even so, we worry. She's not as strong as she once was. Yet she thinks she's invincible."

"What's the convention?"

"She's very excited about going. Apparently, her husband belonged to an online group, and when she went online to cancel the membership, the good people invited her to attend in his place." She laughed. "It's amazing. She interacts with them on the computer like a pro. E-mail and everything. It's hard to believe she's in her eighties."

"What's this group all about?" Mary expected it to be something about crocheting.

"It's about finding your ancestors," Rebecca said.

TWENTY-ONE

———◆◆◆———

I'll take these to Sunday school tomorrow for the bake sale," Ashley said as she popped a large marshmallow into her mouth. "Do you think the nurses would let me take one to Isabella?" She looked up at Mary, her eyes hopeful.

She stood on a chair next to Mary, a big apron tied around her tummy, its ties long enough to go around twice. In front of her, on the counter, was a large rolled-out circle of cookie dough, which Ashley was stamping with a round cookie cutter.

"I think that's a terrific idea," Mary said, "but we'll need to call Isabella's mom and dad and find out if it's okay. They may have to check with the nurses and doctors too. Sometimes people in hospitals have special foods they need to eat to stay healthy."

"Can you call right now?" She looked up at Mary, her eyes pleading. Then she picked up the flour-smudged printout of the recipe Mary had found on the Internet. The picture showed the final product: sugar cookies iced with white frosting, a marshmallow head stuck on in the middle, which brought the snowman to life with thin-piped frosting for eyes, mouth, arms, and buttons.

"I hope they say yes, 'cause I think these are the cutest cookies ever. Isabella would really, really love one of these."

"You keep working on the cookies, and I'll find out." Mary grabbed her cell phone from her purse and walked to the window, her back to Ashley. If the answer was no, she needed to consider how she would handle it.

Amanda Hiller answered on the first ring. Mary told her about Ashley and her cookie making, and asked if they might bring one to Isabella.

She could hear Amanda take a shaky breath. "She spiked a fever this afternoon. Gabriel and I are taking turns with staying by her bedside—and I just happened to step outside her room. They've moved her to pediatric ICU." She was crying softly. "Oh, Mary, I don't know what I'm going to do. It's just so hard.... The doctors are running tests. They think she's somehow developed pneumonia."

"We'll pray right now, for one thing. You're not in this alone," Mary said. "God is watching over Isabella and lots of friends are praying. You know what His Word tells us— there's not a breath we take that God doesn't know about. Her name—and yours—are written on the palm of His hand."

Amanda was still quietly crying when they ended the conversation.

Mary went back into the kitchen and told Ashley that Isabella was having some tests to help her get better and that she couldn't have visitors.

"I think you should make a very special one just for Isabella, though," Mary said, "and we'll put it in the freezer, wrapped in foil, for when she's feeling better. Maybe you could write her a letter and tell her about the cookies and that you've made one for her."

Ashley put her hand over her mouth and giggled. "That's funny. Putting her melting snowman cookie in the freezer." She giggled again. "I bet she'll really like that. But let's make all the other cookies first. I'll save the best and biggest one for Isabella." She scooped the first cookie-dough circle onto the greased baking sheet and then slid the spatula under another.

"Good idea," Mary said, smiling at the seriousness with which this little girl went about her work. And with each breath, Mary sent a prayer heavenward for little Isabella and her mom and dad.

"I'll make one for Aunt Millicent too. She loves everything I make. She loves to listen to me read. We read a book every night. I love books. So does Aunt Millicent."

Mary helped her scoop a few more onto the cookie tray.

"She has to go away on Tuesday."

"Your mother told me about that. I know you'll miss her."

Ashley nodded. "I love her and don't want her to leave. But I'm glad she asked Mom if she could come stay with us for a while."

Mary stopped midscoop. "She called your mother first?" Millicent had specifically told Mary that Rebecca invited her for the visit, not the other way around. It was true that Rebecca invited Millicent to the book chat, but now it seemed she'd caught Millicent in a bit of stretching the truth about the visit itself.

"Yes. It was after Uncle Oliver went up to heaven. She asked my mother if she could come stay awhile because she was so lonesome."

"That must have been exciting to find out you had a visitor coming." But Mary was thinking about the other conversations she'd had with Millicent and Rebecca about this. Did it make a difference if Millicent had asked Rebecca if she could visit, when Millicent had told her that Rebecca had asked her to come? Was it pride that made her stretch the truth? Or was she forgetful?

Or was there another reason she needed to come to Ivy Bay?

If Rebecca didn't invite Millicent, why exactly the rush to get here?

Ashley continued. "We were having dinner. Mommy made spaghetti. After the telephone call, I told Mommy I didn't remember ever seeing Aunt Millicent before, but Mommy said she hadn't seen her for a long, long time and didn't remember her very well. But she remembered her as kind and loving. And she thought I would like her. And I did."

"I'm sure she'll come back to see you soon. She seems to really love it here and loves being with you and your mom."

"She's going someplace to study about her ancestors. It's her maiden name she wants to find out about."

Ashley shook her head, put the last of the cookie-dough circles on the cookie tray, and then Mary carried it to the oven, placed it on a rack, and set the timer.

Mary's heart began to beat faster at a new thought. If Millicent had met people online who were interested enough in her husband's genealogy to invite her to their annual meeting in Weston, could someone from that group be here in Ivy Bay?

Was that the real reason she'd come?

And if so, did any of this have to do with the missing book? She sighed. Or was she just following a white rabbit down the rabbit hole?

———

Mary took Ashley back to the bookshop to meet up with her mom and Millicent, who told her that Cade had stopped by a half-hour earlier to pick up Heidi—on his motorcycle. Mary bit her tongue to keep from saying anything, but just thinking about the young mother-to-be on the back of that thing worried her more with each day that passed.

The three left a few minutes later, Ashley proudly bearing a Tupperware container of cookies, promising to see Mary at church the following morning. Mary wanted to ask Rebecca about the key but decided to wait until she could catch her alone.

She bustled around, straightening books, checking messages on the phone, and putting away some stray pens. She was about to close the shop when she noticed that a notepad had fallen from the counter under one of the stools. She went over to pick it up, and when she did she felt some indentations across the top. Writing. A word or two, and perhaps numbers. Curious, she flipped on the desk light and held the notepad at an angle to pick up differences in shadow and light.

When she still couldn't make it out, she reached in a drawer for a pencil, and holding it very lightly, rubbed the lead across the notepad.

A phone number appeared in white where the lead hadn't touched. Also a name: Rosalind Hicks.

She stared at the phone number for a half second, recognizing it but unable to put her finger on why. Then it came to her in a flash. She grabbed her phone and pulled up her contact list to be sure. There it was, Orris Rathburn.

Her first thought was that he had called and had left word for her to return the call. But she was certain that if Rebecca had taken a message, she would have said. It wasn't like Rebecca to forget to tell Mary anything that went on in the shop while Mary was away. Millicent had asked if she could help around the shop several times, but Mary knew she wouldn't be answering calls.

Then there was the puzzle of this name, Rosalind Hicks. Could there be someone in his business by that name? Only one way to find out. She dialed the number.

Orris answered almost before the phone rang. Mary greeted him and stared at the notepad for a moment, gathering her thoughts. She didn't want to make any unfair accusations, but something strange was going on and she needed to get to the bottom of it. "Mr. Rathburn, did anyone from your office call me?" she finally asked.

"Not that I know of. Why?"

"My employee was watching my shop this afternoon while I was out. I came back to find a notepad with a name and your phone number on it."

"No, as far as I know, no one from here called. On Saturdays, I'm about the only one to venture into the office."

Mary glanced at the name on the notepad. "Do you know a Rosalind Hicks?"

He was silent for a moment, too long a moment, it seemed to Mary. "You said there was a name on the notepad with my phone number.... The name was Rosalind Hicks?"

"Yes."

"Curious," he said. "Very curious indeed."

"Why?" Mary asked, though not unkindly. "Why is it curious?"

"The name is familiar, that's all. Though I can't place it."

———

Mary gave Rebecca, Millicent, and Ashley enough time to arrive home, and then she called Rebecca. Laughter and upbeat classical music poured through the phone when she answered.

"I wanted to follow up on your time at the shop today," Mary said. "I loved spending time with Ashley. Also, I didn't mention it to her, but I talked to Amanda Hiller while Ashley was there, and Isabella has taken a turn for the worse."

"Oh no, I'm so sorry." Rebecca paused, and Mary thought she heard a whispered prayer. "That's such a danger, always," she said, "with transplant patients."

"It's pneumonia. She's in pediatric ICU. I thought you should know."

They spoke for a few more minutes, and then Mary asked, "Did you take a message for me this afternoon?"

"No," Rebecca said thoughtfully. "We had several calls. Mostly just folks wanting to know if the shop was open."

"I found the notepad with a phone number and name on it. Just thought I'd run it down."

"Oh dear, yes, now I do remember! Millicent and Heidi asked if they could use the computer to look up a reading program." She cleared her throat nervously. "I'm sorry. I should have asked your permission."

"Did either of them happen to use the notepad?"

"They might have written down a Web site or something. I'll ask, if you'd like for me to." She paused and then added, "I hope it was okay."

"It was for a good cause," Mary said. She hesitated, then added, "There's something else. Do you know anything about a key that was made off one of our master keys?"

There was a moment of silence before Rebecca spoke. "No. Why?"

Mary thought about giving her the details, then decided to keep it to herself. Too many unknowns right now. Too many unanswered questions. None of them was easy.

"Don't worry," Mary said easily. "I'll explain later."

They hung up, and Mary stared at the notepad, still curious. Maybe it had to do with the reading program Millicent was looking up.

She typed the name Rosalind Hicks into the search engine box and sat back to watch as several Web sites came up. At the bottom of the second page, she leaned closer to make sure she was reading correctly. And then sat back again, astounded.

Rosalind Hicks was the name of Agatha Christie's only daughter.

TWENTY-TWO

---◆◆---

Sunday morning dawned bright and beautiful, though icicles hung from eaves and icy patches dotted the roads. Much of the snow had melted, and had any snowmen been standing, they would have looked much like Ashley's snowmen cookies.

As always, Mary's heart felt great peace as she entered the sanctuary, a sacred peace mixed with the joy of being with her church family.

She took her place in the pew next to Betty, three rows from the front of the sanctuary. A few minutes later, Rebecca and Russell came in and sat beside Mary.

"Ashley couldn't wait to get to her Sunday school class this morning. She's so proud of those melting snowmen." She laughed softly. "That's all she could talk about last night—and this morning." She met Mary's eyes. "Thank you."

"You know how much I love your daughter," Mary said. "We had fun." She looked back down the aisle and then turned back to Rebecca. "Where's your Aunt Millicent?"

"You won't believe this. She invited Heidi and Cade to come with us this morning."

A grin spread across Mary's face. "Did she really?"

"They're coming on the motorcycle, so she's waiting out front for them."

Mary sighed. "I worry so about them riding that thing. There's still some snow on the ground. Icy patches on the road." She breathed a quick prayer.

"Look who's coming." Betty gestured toward the aisle.

Mary turned. Cade and Heidi flanked Millicent as she hobbled down the aisle, tapping her cane along the way, her tremor more pronounced than usual with her effort. But her smile had never been wider. After a few minutes, she settled slowly into the pew behind Mary, the Gilberts next to her.

The service began with the congregation standing to sing "Amazing Grace." As they finished the last verse, Pastor Miles stood up and moved to the pulpit.

"We're changing the order of the service today," he said. "We have prayed weekly for Isabella Hiller through the past several months, but today she needs special prayer. As many of you know, she's awaiting a kidney transplant that will be done at Boston Children's Hospital.

"She's on a waiting list, and though a donor has been found, there's a tangle of red tape involved. We need to keep that situation in prayer, but something even more pressing has come up.

"Isabella was moved to ICU yesterday and is battling pneumonia. I've asked her mother and father to join us today as we pray once again for this child."

The congregation stood as Amanda and Gabriel Hiller walked down the aisle to stand in front of Pastor Miles.

He placed a hand on each of their shoulders and bowed his head.

"Father, You have blessed Amanda and Gabriel with their daughter Isabella. This morning, we bring her before You, mindful of Your never-failing love—for her, for her parents, for us all, and we pray that You would restore her to good health.

"We read in the first book of Samuel, 'I prayed for this child, and the LORD has granted me what I asked of him. So now I give him to the LORD. For his whole life he will be given over to the LORD.' And we take comfort in these words, Father, because we have the knowledge that Isabella is in Your hands, and that nothing that happens to her takes You by surprise, and that there is never a moment when You are not thinking of her, caring for her, and loving her...."

Pastor Miles concluded the prayer and then asked Gabriel and Amanda to give everyone an update on the latest. Mary's heart sank. Isabella's fever was still high, Gabriel said, which concerned her doctors. They would try a new antibiotic that afternoon. He ended by saying, "Thank you for your prayers, for all that you've done through these months. Your love and concern and support mean more than we can ever say."

Gabriel and Amanda left to return to the hospital, and as the service continued, Mary's thoughts remained with the child and her parents' financial need and the outcome if that need wasn't met.

"Lord," she whispered, "give me a clear mind and wisdom.... Especially wisdom."

Mary was in the parking lot heading to her car, Betty trotting along behind, when she heard the roar of an engine. Even before she turned, she knew the unmistakable sound of a motorcycle.

Cade and Heidi came to a halt beside Mary's car. "How about if we all have lunch together at the Black & White Diner?" Cade asked, his wife looking on approvingly.

"Aunt Millicent is coming, and the Masons."

"Our treat," Cade added with a look of pride.

"We would enjoy it," Mary said, although she couldn't ignore the "my treat" comment.

Cade revved the engine again and then said, "We'll see you at the diner."

It was a sweet thought that they wanted to treat the group to lunch. But how could they afford it?

The Murder of Roger Ackroyd cropped up in her mind's eye again. She shook her head and closed her eyes for an instant. *Lord, help me get to the bottom of this mystery once and for all,* she prayed silently. *And soon.*

They asked for a large table at the diner, and after some maneuvering, Rebecca and Ashley sat on either side of Millicent, and Russell sat at one end; Cade, Heidi, and Betty sat on the other side with Mary on the opposite end.

After they ordered, they chatted for a few minutes about the church service. Cade said he'd like to come back to Grace Church, and Heidi, her eyes shining, agreed.

"I want our kids to go to Sunday school," she said. "And maybe I can help in the nursery. I love babies."

"Congratulations on your house purchase," Mary said to Cade.

He flushed. "It's not a done deal yet, but we're hoping it goes through."

"It's a real fixer," Heidi said, smiling at her husband as though he hung the moon. "Cade's as handy as a pocket on a shirt. He can do anything, fix anything you can name." She hugged his arm. "We don't have much furniture or stuff like that, but I know how to sew, so I can make some curtains. I've refinished old furniture before too, and we plan to get some things secondhand to fill up that old house. Plus, Cade's ma and pa have quite a bit of old stuff we can use."

Millicent leaned forward, her weariness showing, her tremor noticeable. "I need to leave Ivy Bay in a few days, but if there's anything you need, I want you to call me."

Heidi's face fell and she reached for the older woman's hand. "When are you leaving?"

"Tuesday," Millicent said. "I would like to stay, but I have a meeting I need to attend." She gave them all a tremulous smile. "But I'll be back...if you'll have me."

As the waitress poured their soft drinks, Mary turned to Cade. "How long until you find out about the purchase going through? That must be unsettling to have to wait and wonder."

He nodded and then swallowed hard. "I've got some things I need to do first."

"He's not even telling me what those things are." Heidi poked her husband playfully in the ribs.

"It's a secret." Cade set his mouth in a straight line and let his gaze drift toward an approaching waitress, plates stacked on one arm, a bottle of ketchup in the other. "I believe our food is coming," he said. "I'm starving. How about everyone else?"

Mary asked Ashley to say the blessing, and after she finished, while the others reached for their hamburgers and fries, she told everyone about the hit that her cookies were in Sunday school.

"I just wish Isabella was better so I could take her one. We prayed for her in Sunday school today. I just know she's gonna be better soon. I always like to think of her being held like a little lamb in the Good Shepherd's arms. We have a picture like that in our Sunday school room."

Rebecca cut her hamburger into four pieces and gave two to her daughter, along with a scoop of french fries.

"Don't forget," Cade said, smiling grandly at everyone, "this is our treat."

TWENTY-THREE

Sunday evening, Mary stopped by the bookshop to pick up the inventory reports that Rebecca had been working on the previous week. She also picked up two new Fancy Nancy books for Isabella, wrapped them in a gift bag with colorful tissue paper, and wrote out a gift card to tuck inside.

It was dark, cold, and windy when Mary locked the shop and walked out to the Impala. Thankful she'd bundled herself in the ankle-length down coat, she wrapped the long woolen scarf around her neck and over her head to protect her ears. According to the forecast, another nor'easter was headed to Cape Cod and would arrive by midday Tuesday. So far the night was clear, though, and the stars twinkled with stunning clarity. The lull before the storm, she thought, but then she quickly pushed the notion from her mind.

She stopped by the hospital and saw Amanda, Isabella's mother, in the lobby. She already knew that the child was too ill to have visitors, so she handed the gift bag to Amanda and gave her a hug.

"Isabella is in our prayers day and night," Mary said.

"Thank you." Amanda smiled through her tears. "She's better tonight. The doctors think they can move her from ICU tomorrow."

"That's wonderful news."

"I'd hoped to have a chance to thank you," Amanda said. "Dad told us how you'd planned to give us the money from your book's sale."

"I'm so sorry," Mary said. "I'd so hoped to help out in some way."

She smiled. "You did without realizing it. It gave us hope that God is watching out for us even when we aren't aware of it. Not a sparrow falls that He isn't aware of it, and our Isabella is worth so much more than a sparrow."

"Amen," Mary said, smiling.

"Just to know you cared that much..."

Mary grabbed her hand and squeezed it. "I'm not giving up. I'm still determined to find the missing book."

Though in her heart, she wondered how.

Oh, Lord, she thought. *It seems an impossible task to me, and it is—without Your help. Please, help me.*

When Mary walked in the front door of her home several minutes later, the scent of roasting chicken with rosemary, thyme, and lemon wafted toward her. She shrugged off her coat, unwound her scarf, and placed them on the coat tree in the entry. She hurried to the kitchen to see if she could help her sister with dinner. She peeked in the oven, closed her eyes, and drew in the pleasurable scent of her favorite green-bean casserole bubbling on a shelf below a golden-brown chicken. Two small baking potatoes seemed to wink at her from their perch on the upper shelf next to the roasting pan.

Comfort food all the way. And how she needed it this night. She could have hugged Betty when she walked into the kitchen. And she did.

"Wow," Betty said. "What's that for?"

"This dinner..." She gestured toward the oven. "Nothing could be better on a cold winter's evening. You've gone to a lot of trouble."

Given Betty's painful arthritis, food preparation wasn't easy for her, which made her gift an even greater blessing.

"Have you finished calling everyone about tomorrow night?" Betty said over dinner.

Mary filled her baked potato with Betty's homemade gravy, refusing to think about the calories and cholesterol. Comfort food was comfort food, and on a cold wintry night, this was exactly what she needed. She could always return to counting calories tomorrow. Or maybe she would wait until the leftovers were gone.

"I need to make a few more calls to remind folks, but I've reached nearly everyone."

"Same time?"

"Seven on the dot."

"You're going early again?"

Mary nodded. "My plan is to repeat exactly what happened last week. Down to the gnat's eyelash. Flashlights in the same places."

"Power off, lights out?" Betty scooped more gravy onto her potato.

"I've asked Chief McArthur to help." Mary had seen him at church and took him aside to ask him the favor. He was more than happy to go along with the plan, expressing regret that he hadn't been able to find the book himself. "He'll be standing by outside with some power company personnel to take care of it at precisely the same time the power went out last week, and he'll keep it off for the same length of time."

Betty smiled. "Pretty ingenious, if you ask me. Are you sure it will work?" She sounded skeptical.

"I'm optimistic."

"Will you bring charges when the thief comes forth?"

"I won't need to if my plan succeeds." She drew in a deep breath and then deftly cut away a juicy portion of white meat that happened to be attached to the wishbone.

"You may need that wishbone tomorrow," Betty said.

"And prayer. Lots of prayer."

TWENTY-FOUR

——◆◆◆——

Mary unlocked the shop early the following morning. She turned on the lights and turned up the heat, set the carrier down, and let Gus out. He went immediately to his food dish in the back room and told Mary in no uncertain terms that it was empty.

She stooped down and gave him a loving rub behind his ears as she poured kibble into his bowl. He tried to purr and eat at the same time and finally gave up on the purr.

Chuckling, Mary went ahead with the business of readying the shop for opening.

The predicted storm had moved in overnight, and the light snow that began at dawn was forecast to last at least twenty-four hours.

As she started a fire at the hearth, she glanced toward the window at the gently falling snow. She'd called last week's attendees about the book chat scheduled for this evening, and all had said they would be there. Heidi had asked if Cade could come with her, and Nigel had asked the same about Leona, and, of course, Mary said yes to both.

If the storm behaved itself and the snowfall remained light, everyone who attended the week before would return.

Word had spread since the previous book chat about the strange disappearance of *Roger Ackroyd*, and she had carefully told each of her suspects about the book, knowing the opportunity to return the book tonight would be evident to them. As she got the refreshment table ready, she wondered if her plan would work.

Millicent and Rebecca arrived a few minutes later. "I need to leave for an hour or so," Rebecca said as her aunt moved across the shop with her cane tapping and sat heavily in the rocker. Gus hopped on her lap and curled up. "I hope it's all right to leave Millicent here while I run to the school. Russell's waiting in the car. We've got a teacher's conference appointment."

"Of course it's okay," Mary assured her.

"She's invited Heidi Gilbert to stop by for a last reading lesson." She lifted her eyebrows as if asking permission.

Mary put her arm around Rebecca to reassure her that the lesson would be perfectly fine. "I'll enjoy Mozart," she said. "In fact, I think I'll play it more often in her honor."

Rebecca gave her a quick nod and ducked out into the chilly morning weather.

It wasn't until a few minutes had passed that Mary realized Rebecca had seemed somehow preoccupied. She was staring through the window, contemplating why, when Millicent startled her.

"You're sure I won't bother you with Mozart playing?" As she talked, she brought out her latest project: a pair of booties for one of Heidi's babies. "I'm making little sweaters to match the booties, though I've started Heidi on a baby blanket with rows of double crochets. That's the easiest for a beginner to learn to crochet."

"Pink or blue?" Mary asked.

"Variegated pastels. It will work for either gender, or both."

Within the hour, Heidi arrived on the back of the motorcycle. Mary walked to the window and watched as Cade kissed his wife good-bye and then waved as he revved the engine and roared off. "I know, I know," Heidi said with a laugh as she removed her helmet. "You don't even have to say it. But the motorcycle's what keeps us both young. I've even been trying to figure out how I can afford to buy him a sidecar for the babies."

Mary caught her hand to her mouth, breathing a prayer. Heidi saw what she was doing, laughed again, and touched Mary's arm. "I'm kidding about that. Besides, knowing how fussy Cade is about that bike, he'd never allow anything to be put on it that wasn't original to the year and make."

"What year is it?"

"It's a 1937 Harley Davidson EL Knucklehead."

Millicent laughed. "Knucklehead?"

"That's its name." She blushed as she walked closer to where Millicent sat crocheting. "And that's what he calls me sometimes, his little Knucklehead. Some women might be offended. But I know how much he loves that old machine, how much time and TLC he's given it. When he calls me that, his voice has a lot of love in it. So I don't mind at all." She sat down next to Millicent. "Do you want me to put on the music?"

Mary went to her computer on the counter as Heidi and Millicent settled into what had become a bit of a routine over the course of the week. Soon, the beautiful sounds of piano concertos filled her shop, mixing with the sound of Heidi's soft voice reading to Millicent. The fire crackled as Mary turned on her computer.

She went immediately to eBay and typed in 1937 Harley Davidson EL Knucklehead. As she waited for the page to come up, the entrance bell tinkled, and she looked up to see Alexa Rose come in.

Mary got up and headed to the entrance to greet her.

"It's good to see you again," Mary said, giving Alexa a small hug. "And great to see you in my shop."

"I've been meaning to pop in and tell you that I enjoyed our visit the other day." Alexa reached in her handbag and pulled out the two Ellis Peters books. "And I have to admit . . . I loved these. Stayed up all night to finish the first one." She handed both books to Mary.

"I'm so glad to hear that. Please, come in, and I'll show you around."

"I can't really say you've made me a convert," she said as she followed Mary into the shop. "I still prefer the older classics." Her eye caught Betty's teapot collection. "May I have a closer look?"

"Of course. They belong to Betty."

She exclaimed over a few, and Mary gave her the history of them.

When they turned toward the back of the shop, Alexa stopped for an instant as if surprised. She quickly recovered, but not before Mary noticed Millicent's expression.

It was a look of recognition.

"Would you like a cup of tea? Come over and meet my friends while I pour you a cup."

"No, thank you," Alexa said. "I need to get back to the inn."

———

A short while later, Mary was still pondering the strange encounter with Alexa, and after a few more customers had come in and needed help, Mary finally returned to her computer. Reading and conversation and Mozart hummed in the background.

She pulled out a notepad and pen. The page she'd jotted notes on beginning a week ago was now filled with notes about her theories.

Sitting back in her chair, she read through each one, taking her time to think through what she'd discovered about all the suspects. So many dead ends. So many things left unexplained.

She thought again about motives and opportunities and how, even if they helped her deduce who the thief was, they meant nothing in a court of law. She needed solid evidence. And all she had were scraps of ideas, dots that didn't yet connect.

And time was running out.

She thought of Isabella and felt a sting at the top of her throat. She swallowed hard. This was no time to cry; this was a time to make her brain work harder than it had ever worked before. For Isabella.

Gus jumped onto the countertop and walked across her keyboard, tail waving high, purring loudly. Then he jumped to her lap, curled, and went to sleep.

She clicked on the Harley Davidson Knucklehead page and gaped as she sat back, realizing the antique motorcycle's worth. Was he just into "little boy toys," not realizing that it was time to grow up and take responsibility for his growing family?

Or was the motorcycle's worth significant in how he was planning to take responsibility for his family? The truth was, she didn't know him well enough to be sure either way.

She was still pondering the young man's character as she jotted down the remaining clues.

1. Note with indented ph number (Orris's) and name (Rosalind Hicks)
2. Rosalind Hicks's identity—Agatha Christie's granddaughter
3. Calendar page with N U A R Y
4. Bit of yarn—likely from one of Gus's toy mice with yarn tails?
5. Photos of tire marks in snow
7. Comb with silver-embossed frame, engraved letters, maybe RH or RW, with 3rd letter unreadable

She held the notebook to the desk lamp and studied it while she sipped her tea. She thought about the comb with the initials RH. She would need to double-check with Chief McArthur, but a smile overtook her face as the realization dawned.

Rosalind Hicks! RH. *The comb.*

She turned to the computer and once more typed in the name on the Google search page, reviewing the sites that listed Rosalind Hicks, Agatha Christie's only daughter.

She jotted down notes in greater detail, paying closer attention than before.

Mary's heart thudded as she went through the rest of the evidence, discarding some, keeping others. Pieces of the puzzle were beginning to fit together. Completely together. A picture emerged. Maybe not the entire picture, but enough for her to put motive, opportunity, and evidence together.

She did one last search, one she never expected to connect to the missing *The Murder of Roger Ackroyd.*

For an hour, she searched through genealogy groups. Local groups. Who was in leadership in the area?

Finally, she found the name she was looking for. "Oh my," she breathed. "Oh my..."

Gus looked up, mildly interested.

She smiled as the impact of her find soaked in.

"I've got it!" she whispered to Gus as she jumped from her chair. "I know who did it."

TWENTY-FIVE

───◆◆◆───

A half hour before the book chat was to begin, towns-people began pouring into the shop. Mary exchanged surprised glances with Millicent who was sitting in the rocking chair by the fire, working on another pair of booties. "I didn't know so many people were invited," Millicent said, wide-eyed.

Mary didn't either. She guessed that word of the book chat had gotten around town. Even Ashley and a few of her classmates had come and were sitting with a group of parents and their teacher Mrs. Jacobs. All for Isabella, Mary realized, though it did change the dynamic she'd planned. A dynamic she'd put in place to catch the thief. How was she to do an exact reenactment of last week's book chat with a host of people and new variables? She whispered a prayer, asking for peace and acceptance of what was to come. Human plans weren't always best, and she smiled as she realized Someone else might have a better plan in mind.

She was still smiling at the wonder of it all when Bob Hiller pulled her off to one side. He was smiling broadly, and suddenly it hit Mary. The phone call Bob had made at the hospital...

"Bob, did you invite all these people?"

He nodded his head humbly. "Not directly. But I did start a rumor....Dorothy Johnson is pretty reliable if you want word to spread quickly." Mary couldn't help but laugh a little, but Bob's expression sobered. "I hope it's okay. See, I explained to Dorothy about how the book was meant to help Isabella and how the thief was still out there. I wanted news to get around town that this book was meant to help a sick little girl. I thought maybe, that way, the thief's guilty conscience would kick in." Little did Bob know that Mary had already been working on that theory for days but with a smaller sample. Bob waved at Dorothy who was pouring herself some tea. "Within hours, people were approaching me, saying that they'll see me at the book chat." He smiled. "I suppose they wonder if they'll be a part of catching a thief. Or perhaps they've come just to show support." Bob looked around at the crowd. "Mostly, I just wanted whoever the sad soul was who stole the book to know they won't get away with it."

"They won't," Mary said to reassure him. "Thank you for your help," she added, although it wasn't exactly how Mary would have defined "help." Mary looked around, blinking with surprise and trying to quickly readjust her thinking about how this evening would go. Still more people squeezed through the door and into her shop. There were couples, oldsters and youngsters, and families.

Betty bustled in then with her Tupperware containers of cookies, stopped dead still, and gaped. Mary knew what was going through her head, and from across the room, she caught her sister's eye. She shook her head, meaning, "Don't you dare go back home and bake more cookies."

Betty grinned and gave her a thumbs-up sign. Then she mouthed, "Pray for loaves and fishes."

Nigel and Leona came up to Mary, each holding a cup of tea. Leona gave Mary a hug. "In case there's no time later for good-byes," Leona explained. "Thank you again from the bottom of our hearts."

As seven o'clock approached, Mary looked around the room. There weren't enough seats, so some of the younger people were sitting on the floor. She noticed that people were breaking cookies into two or more pieces to share, and Betty seemed to have turned into a whirling dervish as she made pot after pot of coffee and heated water for tea in the kettle.

Mrs. Jacobs was standing near the counter, and Ashley had snuggled up beside her. A few of Ashley's friends were with her, and Mrs. Jacobs was holding a box with crayon drawings on the exterior.

Pastor Miles was sitting on the floor next to Bob Hiller. Henry Woodrow was on the opposite side. All three leaned back against a bookshelf.

Dorothy Johnson came rushing through the door just as Mary was about to begin. For the first time in a long time, she didn't search the room for Henry. She quietly took her place near the hearth.

Mary looked out over the sea of faces.

"As you know," she began, knowing full well that soon enough the lights would go out, "this was intended to be the second book chat to talk about Agatha Christie's *Murder on the Orient Express*." She took a deep breath. "But I know that many of you are here because of what you heard about the other Christie book, *The Murder of Roger Ackroyd*. Thank you, from the bottom of my heart. I know that some of you have read the *Orient Express*, and many of you are here in support of the Hillers. For now, let's start with a book chat. Anyone and everyone is free to contribute! Who would like to start?"

Henry got up from where he'd been sitting on the floor. "What I got from this, and from other Agatha Christie books, is the dogged determination of the sleuth to find the one who committed the crime. No matter the danger or discouragement, the idea that justice had to be done was always at the forefront of that character's mind." He met Mary's eyes. "Mary has been in pursuit of justice with getting to the heart of the mystery of this priceless book. Not for herself, not out of curiosity, or for some ego need. She's been dogged in her determination to help a child in need." He smiled at her. "And she wanted to keep it quiet—at least as long as she could—that it was to be a gift to help a child get well."

Mary shook her head slightly. "Well, we're getting a little off track from the story, but I thank you, Henry, for your kind words. Now, let's take another look at—"

Just then the lights went out.

There was an audible gasp.

Someone groaned, "Oh no, not again!"

A general hubbub ensued. Mary could hear chairs scraping and moving, footsteps shuffling.

"Let's stay seated," she said. "Please. Everyone sit down. Bob and Henry, would you grab the kerosene lamp at the back of the shop? Rebecca, grab candles and flashlights?"

Mary heard a few words of complaint about the power company, another about the weather and maybe more winds on the way.

Several minutes passed, and then Bob and Henry returned with the antique lamp. They had just set them down when the lights flickered and went on again.

Holding her breath as everyone else sat down, Mary turned toward the glass-fronted counter near the cash register. It had been cleared of clutter before the book chat started. But now, though no one was near the counter, several boxes were stacked on top of the case, one with crayon pictures, and several envelopes had been left in a basket...as if in offering.

She squinted, searching for *The Murder of Roger Ackroyd*.

TWENTY-SIX

——◆◆◆——

For a long moment, no one spoke, and then Ashley started clapping, jumping up and down in her excitement. "Come and look! Hurry!" Now the whole room filled with applause, and the crowd parted like the Red Sea between Mary and the counter where the gifts had been placed. Ashley, holding her teacher's hand, was still bobbing up and down.

Mary was still trying to make sense of the turnaround when she reached the counter full of gifts. How did her plan to find the book thief take such a strange turn?

"Open this one first!" Ashley picked up the box with the bright crayon drawings. Several of her classmates were laughing and catching their hands to their mouths in excitement as Mary took the gift from her adopted granddaughter.

Mary lifted the lid.

"We did it our own selves," Ashley said. "That's the money I told you about. We've been collecting it from everybody." Mary peered in the box. It was full of pennies, nickels, dimes, and quarters. Several bills were among other folded pieces of paper, colorful drawings, and letters to Isabella. Mary clutched it close to her heart. "It's the most precious gift ever," she said.

234 C~ SECRETS *of* MARY'S BOOKSHOP

Henry came over to have a look and told the children how special a gift it was. "Can I help too?"

The children nodded emphatically.

He pulled out his wallet and emptied every bill he had into the box.

"Hey, pass it over here," someone called from the back of the room.

Mary grinned when she saw who it was. Orris Rathburn. She'd called him to let him know about her plan, once she'd set it in motion. She had no idea that he'd show up. She remembered his concern about Isabella the night he told her of the book's worth, and she blinked back the sting in her eyes as he dropped in an envelope. He gave her a wave, and the donations around the room continued.

"And here," someone called out, waving a check.

"Don't forget us," Cade Gilbert yelled, a wide grin spreading across his face. He waved a check with great fanfare.

"We just today sold the Knucklehead," Heidi called out, her face aglow. "The buyer took it for a test-drive last night. Said he fell in love with it. We can buy our house now!" She patted her stomach. People applauded who didn't even know what she was talking about. Mary loved every minute of it.

It appeared that everyone whose hand it touched put something in. It became more solemn as the box was passed and time went on. Little children dropped in change, others maybe a dollar, very often accompanied by a prayer. Almost like an offering from church, Mary thought.

It reached the Finnians, and after nodding at each other, Nigel pulled out a checkbook, filled out a check, signed it, and dropped it in the box. Leona looked at the number he had written with tears in her eyes and then she passed it to the next person.

For a half hour, the box made its rounds, and when it finally came back to Mary, it was filled to the brim.

"Thank you," she said, almost not trusting herself to speak. "Bob, will you take it to Amanda and Gabriel?"

"There's more!" Ashley was jumping up and down again like it was Christmas. "Remember the bake sale we made melting snowmen for?"

"I sure do," Mary said.

"Well, this next one is for that and a bunch of other things people have been selling this week. Homemade items mostly. We made things at the school cafeteria, and there were homemade blankets, and even Aunt Millicent crocheted some caps for children in the hospital who are sick like Isabella. She has been making them for a year, not knowing what she'd do with them. She had hundreds. People bought them for those little kids, but they donated them to the hospital." She shook a large tin that appeared to be left over from Christmas. It rattled with change.

She gave it to Mary, who pried open the top and peered inside. "Oh my," she breathed. "This is amazing. There are hundreds of dollars in here." She looked out over the group, meeting the eyes of individuals, many who were friends, some acquaintances, some she didn't know. She saw Alexa Rose in the back row and gave her a welcoming smile. She hadn't seen her earlier, so she must have come in through the back door.

Surprisingly, Alexa looked ready to cry. She held up an envelope. "Is it too late to contribute?"

"Not at all," called out several folks.

She passed the envelope forward. When it reached Mary, she noticed the faint scent. Cinnamon and nutmeg. The same scent of potpourri that wafted throughout the Chickadee Inn.

"Thank you," she said to Alexa and then dropped the envelope into the tin.

"And now, ta-da!" Ashley said, lifting a book-sized package from the counter. "I don't know what this is, but somebody put it here with the rest, so it must be for Isabella too."

As soon as she felt the weight of the box in her hands, Mary knew what it was.

Her plan had been for the suspect to return the book to the case, put it in the box she'd left open, and when the lights went on, the guilty one would be seated among the others, no one the wiser. Maybe that wasn't the traditional way to catch a thief, but this time, it was her way. It had to be. She knew she couldn't expose and embarrass the thief. The book was back. That's all that mattered.

Mary knew who did it, but she would never let on to anyone.

She hugged the book, whispering a prayer of thanksgiving. "Everything all right in here?" Chief McArthur said, stepping in from outside.

"Never better," Mary said.

Orris Rathburn came up to Mary, a wide smile on his face. "I'm glad you called earlier, though I wondered how you could be so certain the book would be returned."

"Call it faith," Mary said.

"Well, I believed you. The buyer has been notified, and the money already transferred."

"It has?" Mary couldn't stop smiling. "What about the second appraisal?"

"He decided he trusted my original appraisal. He wanted to make sure the book didn't get away from him again."

"You're taking it to him tonight?"

Orris laughed. "Yes, if you don't mind."

"Mind?" Mary could have hugged him. But instead, she handed him the book and shook his hand.

"It's been a pleasure doing business with you," Orris said as he headed to the front door. "If you ever have another find like this, let me know."

"Actually, I'll be quite happy if I don't." Mary laughed and waved as he opened the door and stepped through.

TWENTY-SEVEN

Snow fell in large lazy flakes as Mary locked the doors of Mary's Mystery Bookshop. The streetlights that lined Main Street cast a golden glow diffused only by the falling snow. She gazed down the street at the old-fashioned buildings, a scene she never tired of. Some had lights in their windows; others were closed for the night.

She stood near her car and looked up into the glorious sky and stuck out her tongue to catch a flake. She giggled, feeling like a schoolgirl. She took in the bookshop, its beautiful storefront, and the teapot display Betty worked on so lovingly.

How blessed she was to be in this place, a place where people cared for one another. With considerable awe, she realized that no one had asked if she knew who it was that took the book. It was as if mercy and forgiveness and unconditional love were part of their DNA.

She started toward the Impala and then stopped as headlights moved through the snow toward her. The vehicle slowed, its tires crunching the snow, and then turned toward the curb to park behind the Impala.

It was Millicent, gingerly driving her four-wheel-drive Jeep Cherokee, a bit weathered and dented. Millicent's head barely showed above the steering wheel.

Mary wasn't surprised.

The sweet, giving little woman she'd come to care for stepped down from the vehicle and walked toward her, tapping her cane with each step.

"I was hoping you'd still be here," Millicent said.

"I was hoping you'd come." Mary gave her a tender smile. "Though I knew it would be hard."

Tears filled the older woman's eyes.

"Would you like to go inside where it's warm?"

Millicent shook her head. "This won't take very long." She took a deep breath, looking up at the falling snow. "It's beautiful, isn't it? What I did—" Millicent began, swallowed hard and then started again. "I never meant for it to go as far as it did. When I slipped into your shop the night of the first book chat, I'd planned to get the book and be gone before you arrived. I never expected you to come in early." She shook her head slowly. "It was supposed to be so easy. I was just going to borrow it and then return it without you knowing.

"You pulled up in your Impala and scared me to death. I'm afraid I was rather clumsy. I just dropped the book and got out of there by the back door. I'd barely made it out when you unlocked the front door and came in."

Mary frowned. "You could have gotten hurt hurrying out through the dark shop."

"I had a penlight. It wasn't much, but it was enough. I was thrilled later, when the lights went out and I had another chance. But I was never alone long enough to get to the box again. Too many people milling around the counter. Especially that Nigel character. I almost thought he was there to do the same thing I was."

"How did you take it?" Mary knew the gist at this point but hoped Millicent would fill in the holes.

"I waited until you left with Heidi to slip back in. I'm so ashamed of all the lies I told—even to my dear Rebecca. She expected me to follow her home that night after the book chat. I told her I needed to stop for gas. Which was true. I did."

"But you added a few minutes to return to the shop and take the book."

She nodded, tears still brimming. Mary reached for Millicent's gloved hands. "And then all week you tried to return the book."

Millicent frowned. "How did you know?"

"I noticed your oversize yarn bag. When I finally put two and two together and figured out it was you, I noticed that it seemed awfully bulky to hold yarn only. And you seemed awfully eager to be alone in the shop." Mary gave her a knowing smile. "Besides, I couldn't imagine you as a thief. A real thief."

Millicent nodded. "Once I realized the awful deed I'd done, I wanted to undo the whole thing. Put the book back and not embarrass myself, or Rebecca, by just handing it to you." She looked away.

Silence fell between them, but Mary waited for her to go on. It wasn't an easy tale to tell.

"I met someone online...," Millicent finally said, "through one of my husband's groups. I trusted her. I'd told the people in this group that I was in financial difficulty..." Her voice broke. "And knowing who I was, who my husband was related to, they...well, she, actually...they all gave me advice I should have taken."

"Advice you *should* have taken?" Mary frowned, now confused.

Millicent nodded. "Yes. If only I had....But first let me tell you how it happened. I came here early, you know. I stayed at the inn the night before I supposedly drove through the windstorm."

"I know."

Millicent's eyes widened. "How?"

Mary began. "Both bridges were down the night you called and said you were on your way. I was investigating someone else I thought might have been involved, checking on her arrival time. When I found out about the bridges, I wondered how you made it across the night of the book chat." Millicent drew in a breath, and Mary put her arm around her. "It's cold. Are you sure you don't want to go inside?"

The older woman shook her head. "I need to finish while I have the courage." She paused, looking up at the falling snow for a moment and then turned again to Mary. "About the key. You probably wonder how I got it."

Mary nodded, though she had a pretty good idea. "It was a copy of Rebecca's. When Rebecca extended the invitation to come here, she told me where to find the house key under her mat on the back porch—in case I got here when no one was home. Well, that's what happened. And then I found other keys hanging on little posts beside the door. One was marked Mary's Mystery Bookshop, so I borrowed it and had a copy made. That's the one I put back in the teapot, hoping that someone would find it but be none the wiser." Her shoulders slumped. "I'm awfully sorry for the trouble I've caused."

Mary drew in a deep breath. "We know how and when you got in. Now tell me about the book," she said gently. "And why."

"I had my reasons, and they were good ones. At least I thought so. I planned to just borrow the book and get my own appraisal. After that, I planned to get an attorney. Make a claim that the book should go to me as one of the heirs of the estate. I'd hoped to return the book before anyone knew it was missing. Then make my claim before you sold it." She dropped her gaze. "I had no idea you'd already found a buyer."

"The claim would have been difficult to prove. Did anyone mention that?"

"Some said it sounded pretty far-fetched and advised against it," Millicent said. "But I was desperate. I panicked when my husband died and left me with huge bills. I was grasping at straws. I'd just found out that he had gambled away our life savings through day-trading."

"And someone gave you advice based on that fear." Mary paused and then added, "Alexa Rose was that person."

Millicent's eyes widened. "Why, yes. It was Alexa. How did you know?"

Mary decided it was better not to go into the details about how Betty had found the dime novels. It had become clear to Mary that Alexa had a love not for antiques but for ancestry research. She smiled as she gave Millicent the abridged version of the story. "I found a bookmark notation in Alexa's inn, with the Web site of your ancestry research group. After I discovered your connection to Rosalind Hicks, yours and

Alexa's mutual interest in ancestry clicked. Alexa had been acting as if she was hiding something all week. Now I know what it was."

Millicent let that sink in for a moment, her eyes shining bright in the streetlight. "That's some sleuthing," she said, her admiration clear. Then she sighed. "Alexa said that I might have a claim to the book because of my husband's relationship to Agatha Christie's daughter's estate. She knew my husband had discovered this while searching for his ancestry online." She stopped speaking and frowned. "How did you know about Rosalind Hicks?"

"You wrote it on a piece of paper and left the indentation for me to lift with a few light strokes of a pencil. When I Googled the name, I discovered who she was, her connection to Agatha Christie, and then matched the initials to a comb I found."

"Comb?"

Mary reached into her coat pocket and pulled out the picture she'd taken with her phone. "Is this yours?"

"It was my husband's." Millicent swallowed hard. "Alexa called me the same day your appraiser was here. It seems he bragged to a waitress at a diner outside town about this priceless book he'd just seen. She heard about it and called me immediately. The word—at that time—was that the book was appraised at a much higher price. He may have been trying to impress her. Or it was a case of the rumor becoming bigger and better with each telling." She shrugged. "I fell for it."

She dropped her head. "But as I mentioned earlier, Alexa's plan was different than mine, and I wished a thousand times this week that I had followed her advice. She just wanted me to tell you that I might have a claim to it and ask if you might delay selling it." She looked up as the tears rolled down her cheeks. "It was my idea to take the book and have it appraised—without anyone being the wiser—and then return it."

So Alexa hadn't urged Millicent to take the book? Mary was relieved to hear it.

Millicent dropped her head, and this time, the tears spilled. "When my husband died, he left me strapped with a big house full of gorgeous furniture and not a penny to take care of it. He'd mortgaged our home to the hilt. Apparently, he'd voiced his woes to his online friends, because when I found these groups and told them of his death, I planned to discontinue membership. But it seems everyone but me knew of our debt and also of the claim he might have to the Agatha Christie legacy.

"Everybody in the ancestry group is so caring. They really had good advice and were so worried about me. I don't think any of them would do something purposefully to harm another." She drew herself up tall. "I can't blame anyone else but myself for this."

She turned to Mary. "Please don't be harsh in your judgment of Alexa. She knew what I did and that I was trying to return the book. She finally said that she would tell you herself if I didn't—and soon." She smiled. "She didn't say it as a threat. She was just trying to help me do the right thing. The day she came by with the Cadfael books, I expected her to tell you. But she saw Heidi, and I guess she didn't want to embarrass me. I believe she came tonight to make sure the book ended up where it was supposed to."

"How did you know you'd have the chance to put it back tonight?"

Millicent smiled. "I'm a mystery buff. I figured out what a good sleuth—*you*—would do. You'd recreate the crime scene down to the gnat's eyelash. Power outage and all. I was ready." She tilted her chin upward, and the sparkle came back to her eyes.

"How about Rebecca? Have you told her?"

Millicent shook her head. "I will before I leave. I wanted to tell you first."

They both looked up at the falling snowflakes for a few minutes, and then Mary said, "I want you to know I forgive you, Millicent. And you're welcome to come back to the bookshop anytime. I'd love to have you help other young people with their reading." She smiled at Millicent. "And you have another gift you may not be aware of."

Millicent looked puzzled.

"Giving of yourself to others. You've only been here a week, but in that week, you've changed lives. You've given your time and energy—and love—to Rebecca, to Ashley, to me, and especially to Heidi. Her life is richer because of what you gave her."

They hugged. "Come back soon, friend," Mary said. "You'll always have a home here in Ivy Bay."

Mary had just walked in the door when she received the call she'd been waiting for.

"You'll never guess where I am," Bob Hiller said.

Mary grinned. From the background noise, she knew, even before Bob told her. But she didn't want to spoil the moment. "Where?"

"I'm with my family," Bob shouted to be heard above the noise of the medevac helicopter. "We're about to get on a helicopter and fly to Boston Children's. I don't know how they finagled a ride for this old grandpa, but I couldn't be happier."

After another moment of helicopter background noise, he added, "Thank you, Mary, for everything."

"Tell them all it was a gift of love from the beginning," Mary said, her tears flowing. "And tell Isabella..."

"Yes?"

"Tell her to enjoy that ride."

ABOUT THE AUTHOR

Diane Noble is an award-winning author of more than two dozen novels—mysteries, romantic suspense, historical fiction—and nonfiction books for women, including three devotionals and an empty-nest survival guide. She was lead author for the popular Guideposts series Mystery and the Minister's Wife, contributing six books. *By Word of Mouth* is her seventh mystery for Guideposts. She is currently writing the first book in her new mystery series The Professor and Mrs. Littlefield, due to be released in September 2013. For more information about Diane, you can stop by her Web site, www.dianenoble.com "like" her Facebook page, www.facebook.com/BooksByDianeNoble, or follow her on Twitter (@dianenoble). She loves hearing from her readers!

A CONVERSATION WITH DIANE NOBLE

———◆◆———

Q: *What draws you to Mary's Mystery Bookshop as a writer?*

A: There is something about a small town setting that's very unique. Add a bookshop and it gets even better! I almost feel as though I can walk through the door of Mary's Mystery Bookshop and immediately feel at home. There's a warmth about the shop itself that I love.

Q: *Which character in the series do you most relate to?*

A: In many ways I relate to Mary the most. But I also admire Betty because of how she handles her rheumatoid arthritis with courage, an uncomplaining spirit, and stamina. She doesn't make a big deal of it and doesn't want others to, yet we know it's always with her. I love how Mary quietly steps in to help her sister when she's having a bad day. I have Parkinson's disease, and I found that while working on *By Word of Mouth*, I became more aware of others who live with incurable diseases. It's my prayer to become more like Mary, helping, encouraging, and honoring those courageous ones in my life.

Q: *What do you hope readers will gain from the books you write in this series?*

A: I hope readers will find my books entertaining, yet also filled with warmth and storylines and characters that bring smiles and maybe a chuckle or two even as the whodunit unfolds. It's always my prayer as I sit down to write every morning that a story line or character, or even a Bible quote, a snippet of a sermon or prayer, will be just what a reader needs while he or she is reading my book.

Q: *Mary loves to make new ice-cream flavors and enjoys reading mystery novels. What are some of your hobbies?*

A: Lately, I've gotten a little more serious about my photography. But I have the most fun using my photos to make scrapbooks and albums for my granddaughters. Besides playing with my little granddaughters (my very favorite thing to do!), I love playing my piano, reading, and cooking—especially trying out new recipes.

Q: *Mary's two favorite confidants are her sister Betty and her old friend Henry. Who are your greatest confidants?*

A: I'm blessed to have some very special friends in my life, especially two women who have been my best friends since we were four years old. Through the years, we've cried together and laughed together. We've held hands through great sorrows, health crises, and the stresses and joys of raising children. We pray for one another daily—more often if needed. Our friendship is based on the One who loves us as no other can, and we reflect that love to one another.

Q: *Please tell us about your family!*

A: My husband is a retired history professor who loves the great outdoors and four-wheeling in our Jeep Wrangler. We're proud of our family, which includes one daughter who's a career girl engaged to be married and another daughter who's married with two young daughters and a part-time career. And of course, I must mention our cats, Percival and Merlin, who allow us to live in their home.

CHICKEN DIVAN

4 deboned chicken breasts
2 (10 ounce) packages frozen broccoli
2 cans cream of chicken soup (or one each, cream of chicken and cream of mushroom soup)
1 cup mayonnaise
1 teaspoon lemon juice
½ teaspoon curry powder
1 cup shredded cheddar cheese
2 tablespoons melted butter
½ cup bread crumbs

Precook chicken and broccoli. Spread broccoli in casserole dish, then place chicken on top. In a separate bowl, combine soup, mayonnaise, lemon juice, and curry powder. Pour on chicken. Sprinkle cheese and buttered crumbs on top. Bake at 350 degrees for twenty-five minutes.

FROM THE GUIDEPOSTS ARCHIVES

◆◆◆

It was probably the gloomiest birthday of all my twenty-three years. I had ten dollars to buy my birthday present. Things were tight at home where I lived while attending seminary. Dad had died unexpectedly a little over a year ago, and my mother, three younger brothers and I were barely making ends meet. God, it seemed, not only had forgotten my birthday but everything else about me these days.

Then I saw it, a shop selling used books. It was a sight no young seminarian could resist.

As I browsed the shadowed shelves, some ancient leather-bound volumes on a lower shelf caught my eye. Squatting down, I pulled one out and gingerly opened it to the title page. I held in my hands, "Job to Solomon's Song, Adam Clarke's Commentary." I withdrew another. "The Practical Observations of Rev. Thomas Scott, DD, with extensive Explanatory, Critical and Philological Notes." The type had been set in Brattleboro, Vermont, in 1836.

I tucked the two books under my arm and reached for more. There was a Wesley's Commentary and then two others, five different commentaries in all. I felt I could use them in my seminary studies. The price seemed a bit steep at two dollars per volume, but I paid at the checkout counter.

Two hours later, as I sat down to dinner, one of my brothers bounded down the stairs.

"Tom," he said, waving a yellowed newspaper clipping, "you may really have something in those old books you just bought." He thrust the clipping into my hand. "I found this stuck in among the pages."

I read the fragile newsprint closely. The long-ago reporter claimed that the bound proof sheets to Wesley's Commentary on the New Testament had disappeared half a century before from a university library in his city. The volume, he wrote, could be distinguished from the first edition by numerous word changes by the author, John Wesley, in his own hand. The reporter went on to list some of the changes.

I rose from the table, my heard pounding. A Wesley's Commentary had been in my stack!

I rushed up the stairs. Any doubts I had melted away as I turned the pages. The changes were all there. Handwritten notes between author and printer crowded the margins. I started in awe at the original handwriting of John Wesley!

The task ahead now was to establish legal claim to the document, prove authenticity, and get an appraisal. I thought it over and sent it to a New York concern where they appraise and auction off antique books.

Months went by. Then a letter arrived from Parke Bernet Galleries in New York City. They had sold Wesley's Commentary to the highest bidder for $5,500. Enclosed was a check.

God had not forgotten my birthday. But His monetary gift served to illuminate a much greater gift; the faith that if I trusted Him, He would lead me into paths of unbelievable fulfillment.

Thomas B. Haughey
San Juan, Texas